2/23/20

Smoke Ring Day

To Russell

For our many years of fighting the good fight!

With appreciation

Andy Fisher

7.00

Smoke Ring Day

Andrew Fisher

International Psychoanalytic Books (IPBooks)
New York • IPBooks.net

Published by IPBooks, Queens, NY Online at: www.IPBooks.net

Cover art by the author.

ISBN: 978-1-949093-48-3

Table of Contents

Acknowledgments

To Lyndy: My life companion, support, editorial advisor and implementer, who understands, loves and accepts me because of and despite who I am.

To Liza: My daughter who always wished she could have grown up in the time of the Beatles.

To Alex: My son who called me a hippie burnout. Now, he'll know why.

To Larry: My younger brother who had the good sense to not follow in my footsteps.

To Jim: My older brother: We're even!

PART ONE

CHAPTER 1

Tennis

The thing I remember most about that day was how muggy it was, a hazy ninety degrees, the day before Labor Day Sunday. My father and I drive to my high school where we meet Rick and his dad, Irwin. Our fathers come to watch us play, Rick against me in the championships: the thirteen and under tennis finals of the City of New Rochelle. The thing is, with Rick and me, we are best friends. All the way back to the second grade. We used to play ping-pong for rulership of the solar system. Eight-year-olds with some powerful ambition.

Getting ready for our pre-match warm up – with his wood tennis press and Tad Davis plastic cover – Rick is silent and focused, twirling his racquet before dropping it onto the grandstand. He's in whites, with Jack Purcell tennis sneakers – you know the kind, with the blue rounded stripe at the toe. Me, I have my red Lacoste shirt. The rest, all white, including my Keds low top sneakers, and my trademark hanging out shirttail. A plastic cover over a Tad Imperial racquet. 1963 – the days when wood reigned. Rick's dad and my father exchange greetings. Rick and I nod silently to each other, with menacingly grim and determined glares mixed with fear. Me, typically impatient, thinking, "Let's just play. Let's get on with it."

After winning the toss, I serve and quickly take the first game with sizzling forehand smashes down the line. Using similar shots, I break Ricky's serve, darting out to a four to one lead before he can catch his breath. My shots, forehand and backhand, go my way. I feel loose and relaxed. The first set is mine, six to one. Rick's shell-shocked, but only temporarily. Returning to the sidelines, he and his dad exchange only a few words. My dad brims with excitement. Me, I'm three feet off the ground. My dad, exclaiming with pride, "Way to go, brother."

Second set. Rick regains his bearings. Always a finesse player, he begins doing his usual thing, the fuck. He slows down the pace of the match, allowing him to recover the precision of his ground strokes. It also wears me down. His placements show smartness and consistency. Six to two, Rick.

Whoever wins the third set takes the match. I knew it would come down to the wire. And here we are in set three. My serve and forehand are back, so is my aggressiveness. I force the pace. Take risks. I rush the net over and over. And once again, Rick, thrown off guard, is down five games to two.

My serve now. Sky-high, I can taste it. Only one more game and I'm the champ. Tension, tongue-tightening time. I double-fault, uncustomarily, on two serves in a row.

Hit out on two other shots, and it's five to three. Flubarooney. Rick serves out his game at love with two aces, his first of the match – two aces with steam on them,.

It's five to four. My serve. Sticky and grimy. I can taste the salty sweat around my mouth as I serve, sensing the surge of temper bubbling up behind my panic. Cursing and grimacing after every shot, my adrenaline is flying. Nerve-wrack alley. The points get longer. We both get a lot more cautious with our shots, not wanting to make a mistake. I can manage this kind of tennis for only so long before my impatience takes over, which it does. Today is no different. Unforced errors. FUCK.

During points, my father begins to yell out from the grandstands – "Cross court him, Arn," – as if he's at a baseball game or boxing match. Already upset and pent-up, I lose even more concentration. I lose my serve again and it's five to five.

Rick serves. Every shot is slow, high and deep as possible. Points lasting minutes. Both of us staying in the backcourt, hitting high lobs. Nobody is rushing net. My father, standing and shouting, "Cross court him, Arn. Cross court him, brother." Frazzled, I yell back—"Shut up." Blown up, sky-high. After ten deuce games, Rick dink shots a winner at net outlasting me for a six to five lead.

My serve, to tie the match. It's over! I'm spent. Concentration gone. I double fault the first two points and then, suddenly, waking up, hit two forehand volleys down the line for winners, thirty all. Then Rick returns a sizzling first serve past my backhand, rushing net for a winner: match point. Me, yelling obscenities at myself, wild with self-hate. I get my serve in. Rick hits to my backhand, a two-handed Cliff Drysdale type. I hit a high lob over Rick's head. He returns to my forehand. I dink to his backhand. He lobs. And I return... just over the back-court line. Game-Set and Match. 1-6, 6–2, 7–5. I rush to net, mechanically shake hands with Rick, head down, not meeting his eyes. I walk away.

"You played a great match, Arn. You nearly got 'em. You're a great tennis player. Never say die. You guys played a great match." My eyes riveted to the ground, I can't look at my father or Rick. All I can muster is a, "Let's get out of here."

While driving to the pizza joint, he talks to me about the match. I'm choked up, heavy with disappointment, fuming.

"You didn't cross court him enough," he repeats several times in his postmortem analysis. "You nearly had 'em. That Rick is a great player though. He just wore you down. You're a never-say-die guy, Arn. What a competitor, Arnie Brucher."

I can barely speak, mostly just nodding or grunting, and giving one word answers while I scarf down my two slices during the drive home. As soon as we hit our driveway, I bolt through the front door and head straight upstairs to my bedroom, close the door and jump on the bed, landing on my back. Alone at last.

CHAPTER 2

Labor Day

The screech of the screen door. Front door slamming. The march up the stairs. Mom hears it all. She knows the score.

Dad comes into the kitchen. She's doing the crossword, drinking instant coffee and smoking her Lark cigarette. "What happened?" she calls out, concerned.

Dad: "He lost. It was a heartbreaker. Three sets.

He had him beat, 5–2 in the last set and then – bang, lost 7–5.

He blew it. And blew up at me, too. He got really mad at me."

Mom: "What did you do?"

Dad: "Well, I was excited, telling him to cross court. He yelled at me for coaching him. I guess he just cracked."

Mom: "You know how much he wants to win and for you to be proud of him. You know, Milt, you're too tied up in their matches, Arnie's most of all."

Dad: "I can't help it. I love them. I want them to win, to succeed."

Mom: "Yeah, but Arnie... he's so sensitive. Your bearing down on him just doesn't help."

Dad: "Yeah. You're right. But the boy's lazy. He doesn't have motivation. Needs a kick in the ass. But he really did play his heart out today."

Mom: "What's he doing now?"

Dad: "Up in his room. Probably sulking. He's upset."

Mom: "Poor kid. This championship meant a lot to him, too. That Ricky Seidlman always seems to outsmart him. They're so evenly matched. Arnie gets upset and your reviews of his performance just makes it worse. Do me a favor, Milt, lay off. Promise me that – will you?"

Dad: "I'll try." He gets up from the table, grabs the Times and walks off with his business section to the living room.

In my room on my bed, face up, I'm staring at the ceiling, tracing the cracks in the white paint, filled with self-reproach. Then it's only anger. Enough. Enough with trying. Fuck winning. No more. Enough of this. No more. I'm paralyzed. It's just too much. And what it means to him. Him. No more. Eventually, I fall asleep to Cousin Brucie's screeching voice playing the top 40's in a loop.

The next day, Labor Day night, Mom, Lew, my younger eight-year old brother and Dave, my seventeen-year old older brother are all eating dinner – dry baked chicken. I notice an envelope under Dad's empty plate. As the rest of us are finishing up, Dad signals his arrival by honking that little beep horn of his Renault. We can hear the garage door open and the purring motor of the Renault settle down for the night.

Dave, tense and excited, looks at Mom. Dad bounds upstairs to the kitchen with his usual cheshire cat smile and big greeting: sunny smile, head to one side, clearly glad to be back with his family as he heads upstairs to wash and change. And, in a snap, he's at the table. Looking down at his just served baked chicken, brown rice and broccoli, he notices the envelope.

"What's this?" he asks no one in particular. And no one says anything as he slices open the envelope. Inside there are twelve 100 dollar bills attached to a note, "From Dave." Dad counts out the money, slowly, methodically, like a cashier at the racetrack. He pockets the dough and then, with his typical curtness, mutters, "I made more than this in half a day's work today." Scooping up some rice, he continues, directing his comments to Dave, "Let this be a lesson to you, brother, about the value of an education. Brains beats brawn." Putting his head down, he begins his frenzy of mechanical eating, as if he's the Charlie Chaplin character on the conveyor belt in "Modern Times."

Dave is silent, crestfallen. Hurt and enraged, his eyes redden. You see, Dave has worked his ass off that summer parking cars at the local beach club in south New Rochelle. Hustling, glad handing, trying to extract as much tip money as possible to help out with his tuition for the fall at NYU, not a cheap school to attend by any measure.

Mom rolls her eyes and looks away. She's ashamed and disgusted by Dad and in pain for Dave. Dave remains silent, only managing to shake his head in disbelief, missing Milt's gaze, while Dad scarfs down the dinner. A sickening sight.

For me, it's happening again. In open-mouthed incomprehension, I'm in awe. What I've just witnessed is confirmation of a new understanding of what's been growing over the last few days. Caring, trying: it means nothing. It just doesn't pay. You can't win.

As soon as the dishes are cleared, I dart upstairs to my room, close the door, turn on the radio. "Murray the K. WINS1010 on your dial." I resume my position, face up, on my back, staring into space. Tomorrow is the first day of school, the beginning of the fall semester – eighth grade.

CHAPTER 3

Bogey

An hour of lying down with Murray the K is about as much as I can take. The house is pretty quiet now. Dad and Mom, in their bedroom watching Gary Moore on TV. Dave, on the phone in his room talking to his girlfriend Louise, no doubt filling her in on the calamity that has just occurred. No doubt garnering sympathy. After all, who in their right mind wouldn't be sympathetic to what's just befallen him? Lew is in his bedroom sorting out his Topps baseball cards. All clear. I can now make my move. Downstairs, through the kitchen. With my pretzels and a bottle of ginger ale, I lope into the den. My best friend, the Zenith black and white TV is waiting for me. It's as if he's been missing me. I turn to Channel 5.

The announcer recites, "Tonight, the 'Maltese Falcon' on Movie Greats." This is not a movie that I'm familiar with, and until now only have a passing awareness of who Humphrey Bogart is. Immediately, I am catapulted to Bush Street in San Francisco, circa 1930. I'm in the offices of Spade and Archer, private detectives, where a certain Brigid O' Shaughnessy has arrived to see Mr. Spade.

Spade: "Send her in, Effie darling," as he lights up a cigarette he's just rolled. The smooth way he handles Brigid. Sam Spade. Private eye. So assured, confident, in control, sardonic. And then Peter Lorre – that cool weirdo – comes in. That bizarre dynamic between them, Cairo (Lorre) and Spade (Bogart). And then soon after the fat man, Sydney Greenstreet. The tone, the confident way Bogart handles the cops, how he talks with women, his secretary, his dead partner's wife and, especially, the way he deals with the "bad guys" – so cool, so Bogart.

I'm blown away. He's got it. So calm. Composed. Together. Plays by his own rules. His own code. Half in, half out, between the law and the underworld. The way he handles the cops and the crooks with such ease – comfortable with the ways of both sides. After two hours watching Spade operate, I know who I want to be. Bogart. The way he squints, smoking a cigarette, holding the end between his index finger and thumb. This guy is it. Bogart. Now I know how to be. No more Mr. Earnest. No more Mr. Shy. No more Mr. Sweet. No more Mr. Intense. No more Mr. Competition. No more myself. I'm done with that .

"Where does it get you?" I ask myself in my best Bogart (brand new me) tone. No-where. No mas. From now on, I'm tough. Reveal little. Stay in control. Keep them all off balance. Yeah, it's gonna be great. I can't wait for school tomorrow, where I get to try out the new me. After jerking off twice, I fall into a deep sleep thinking,

"Yeah, Bogey jerks off," I assure myself. "Sometimes he just wants to be alone with his thoughts and fantasies, unencumbered by dames. Yeah, Bogey probably jerked off with the best of 'em."

CHAPTER 4

Mac and Mark

One month later, in early October, I'm in the boys' locker room changing after an intramural flag football game. I'm quarterback. The opposing quarterback, Mac, whose team we have trounced 21-7, approaches me. I know Mac from Little League and playground tackle football. He's the best white athlete in the eighth grade, even better than me. And I must say in all due modesty, that's saying something.

"Good Game, Bruch," he says. "Say, we're having a poker game at Skip's house Friday night. Why don't you come over and play? We play, nickel, dime, quarter—5 and 7 card stud, high low. Interested?"

"Definitely. Can I bring my friend Mark?"

"You mean Krapola? Yeah. Definitely, he's cool . That'll make four and I'll tell Ronnie M. and Stu and Ronnie F. to come, too. That'll make seven. Good for high/low games. Come over to Skip's at 7:30. His parents will be gone by then. We'll play till 11. They're gonna be in Manhattan. OK?"

"Yeah," I say. "Definitely. And I'll tell Mark."

"Cool."

So, the next day at lunch, I pass the news to Mark, who's generally up for anything, despite the studious pose. That Mark: straight A student without working up a sweat. Good athlete, very affable. As I predicted, Mark's up for it. So now we're seven at Skip's for "big time" north end New Rochelle poker. The next day, after school, Mark and I join forces and whip Mac's team again in intramural flag football 28-0. Mark and me, the invincible combo. The rest of the week passes uneventfully. It's junior high. Boring as shit. I show up, do my hour of Math and English homework, don't read my Science homework, read three times as much as I'm supposed to in Social Studies-type books, as usual, and spend the rest of my time at night hunting for Bogart movies on the tube. "Tonight on Movie Greats: 'The Petrified Forest,' with Leslie Howard and Bette Davis, featuring Humphrey Bogart as Duke Mantee- World Famous Killer."

CHAPTER 5

Skip's (Double Chicago)

Friday night my father drives me over to Skip's house doing his usual third degree, putting me through my paces as he drives. "Who's gonna be there? What're you guys gonna do? Not smoking cigarettes, I hope. No gambling, I hope?"

Me: "Come on Dad – we're just gonna hang out and watch the hockey game. It's no big deal, alright? Cut me some slack."

I keep my answers short, terse and vague. I let on nothing. I reveal nothing. Like the boys on the dock say (according to the movie "On the Waterfront") the code is D and D (deaf and dumb). You don't know nothing! After the ten minute drive, Milt drops me off. I walk in to six guys already in play. There's Mac and Mark on one side of the table, the two Ronnies, Stu on the other side and Skip, the host, visor in tow at the head of the table. Jews all. Ready to play.

The Skip Man, sporting his white visor, is a determined wise ass. Stu, dark, handsome chiseled. Ronnie F., loose, cherubic-faced, jocular. Ronnie M., loquacious, gaunt and affable. Mac, barbaric, focused, intent on winning. Mark, teddy bear-like, droll, skeptical, uninvolved.

These characters are all new people for me with the exception of Mark who I have known since fourth grade Hebrew School. Skip quickly introduces me to some new poker games that I'm not familiar with. The best and most interesting of the lot, a little ditty called "Double Chicago". In a nutshell, Double Chicago is a 7-card stud poker game. In order to win the hand, you need to have the best hand and highest spade not exposed (in the hole). Split pots, i.e., (high hand, high spade) keeps the hand going. The game encourages staying in the hand because it's difficult to attain the highest hand and highest spade at the same time. Anyway, I lose five bucks after forty five minutes with one game of Double Chicago and then I'm out. Ronnie F., Mark and Mac are also tapped out, leaving Skip, Ronnie M. and Stu still in the game.

There's nothing to do waiting for the survivors to finish their game. Mac turns on Skip's stereo putting "Free Wheeling Bob Dylan" on the turnstile. "A Hard Rain's Gonna Fall" standing out in particular. He offers me a Marlboro, my first cigarette ever, which I accept. We alternate between watching the New York Ranger hockey game and spacing out listening to Dylan's plaintive, grating, angry lyrics. What a voice. Gruff and off-key. Sort of like a combination of a mad dog and an off-pitch cantor. Blasts out those lyrics like he's delivering the world a spanking. You can just tell he's not happy about the way things are and he's not holding back whether it's about the situation with Blacks in this country, poor people or simply the way people act toward each other on a day to day basis. I've never heard anything like it before, on record or radio. I am mesmerized, despite being put off by his voice- not exactly easy listening.

Mac, whose father works in the music business assures me that Dylan's the next Elvis, only better, with something to say. Mac's parents are kind of Bohemian/Commie types- real left wing. They make my liberal parents look like Republicans, if you can believe Mac's rendition.

The poker game survivors continue their play. To wile away the next few hours waiting for them to conclude their game, Mac, Ronnie, Mark and I turn onto Dylan and sample the glories of Marlboros. I practice my newly learned Bogart style of smoking cigarettes as the place becomes a swirl of grey smoke. I ponder, and am pleased with the new experiences I'm having: gambling, smoking, listening to Dylan with my new found friends. Firsts, all in one night. Heady stuff.

CHAPTER 6

Jews, Blacks and Italians

Midway into January, 1964. The beginning of second semester eighth grade. The Beatles invade America, dominating the top 40 charts with "I Want to Hold Your Hand" and "She Loves You." Mac and Mark become good friends with each other that year. Stu Gold, too, becoming friends with all of us.

Stu, Mac and I are hall monitors. We volunteer because we know it will let us get us out of class five minutes early and go in five minutes late. So we're happy to have the assignment. Anyway, Stu had been going out with this girl Marcia for about three months that year before they broke up. Typical for my crowd then. Stu and Marcia were both Jewish kids, like most of my friends then. One day, the three of us are shooting the shit while on line, keeping the students to the right in the halls , when Mac and I notice Stu has turned several shades of red. I mean beet red. We are about to ask him what's the matter, when I see Marcia walking past with Jack Fresco, the leader of the Italian greasers, with Marcia wearing, of all things, a cross around her neck. Before I know what's happening, "WHORE" bursts out of the mouth of my purple-faced friend. Then, just as suddenly, Jack Fresco comes out with, "I'm gonna kick your kike ass, motherfucker. See you in the lunchroom, fourth period. You're dead."

Whew. Scared, worried and excited, we wait for Stu to calm down. Then I say to Mac, "Now what? We can't back down." Mac, never needing an excuse for bellicosity, replies with the utmost assuredness, "I'm ready."

Stu: "I'll kill that greaser bastard."

I, somehow the calm one here, mutter, "Wait a minute guys. It's not like we're experienced fighters or nothing. Fresco and his crew, they don't give a shit. They could care less 'bout school and they love to fight. Hey, wait a minute—I know what to do, I'll talk to the Little Brothers. They like me. Maybe they'll provide cover. Anyway, they hate those greasers too, you know."

Mac and Stu nod passively, knowing what I'm saying makes sense but embarrassed to admit that we need Black guys to back us up. I don't care. I just want to win. And I know that backup from the Little's et al. would guarantee it. So during P.E., I stop Mark, one of the main Little's, as we're on the way to the basketball court and tell him what is going on. Right away, no hesitation, he says, "You got it, man. I always hated Fresco. We'll be there. No problem, Jack."

12:30 PM. Lunchtime. Fourth period. Italians, at their usual east wing spot. Jews, at our usual west wing area. The Blacks are patrolling in the north nook. Fresco, with an entourage of twelve trailing behind him, walks toward the Jews, eyeing Stuart. They're all wearing black leather jackets and white tee shirts. I'm with Stu, Mack, and Mark. And we're all scared. The lunchroom is suddenly and deathly quiet and solemn as Jack edges closer to Stu. With Jack about three feet away, I'm quaking in my boots. We're outnumbered and completely outmatched.

After what feels like hours, suddenly, out of nowhere, a commanding voice is yelling at Jack Fresco. It's Mark Little, backed by fifteen of his friends. He's yelling to Fresco,

"Come on Jack, take that next step. I can't wait to get a piece of you."

After an eternity, or maybe two seconds, seven whistles go off at once. First, the custodian and then, Vice Principal Toyota racing to the scene, pushing their way through the crowd of kids. The custodian, arriving first, pushes Stu and Jack away from each other. The rumble's over. No one is sent home. Fresco and Stu are called to the office. Neither are given a suspension or letter home. Both get detention.

Vice Principal Toyota, officious and threatening, barks, "You boys better watch it. I will not tolerate gangs or fighting in this school. Period. Now go back to your areas."

The Italians go back to their side of the lunchroom. The Jews and Blacks stay together in the west wing for a while, schmoozing, joking and low-fiving at their successfully executed two-on-one fast break. Jewish girls and Black girls view the scene from a distance, commenting in a low inaudible hum. Maybe they're making snide comments about boys fighting. Who knows what the girls are thinking? Who cares? We won, at least we would have. That's what I care about. A great moment.

CHAPTER 7

The Track

I don't care what anybody says, that day was a great triumph. A victory of strategy, alliance over stupidity. From that day on, we wouldn't be intimidated by the Italians. We knew it and they knew it. And now they even had a grudging respect for Stu and Mac, and especially for me. It made us, Mac and me, kind of cocky. Feeling our oats.

With the gambling, we decided to up the ante – adventure-wise. A few months later, in May, through a friend of Mac's older brother, we moved up to the racetrack. Harness racing to be precise. At night. More action. More than a bunch of levels in risk taking that we had been into so far. Well beyond nickel and dime poker at Skip's.

Sol Danceway was our guide, mentor. A close friend of Mac's older brother from high school, he was living at home as a freshman at CCNY while the rest of his high school mates went away to school. He'd inspire us with tales of his wins and losses, near misses, this and that. Sol could talk. The stories he told of betting forays had the air of romantic adventure. We couldn't get enough. To get us motivated, posing as a booster for Yonkers Raceway, our home racetrack, he'd intone, "Ladies and Gentlemen: You've got to be there. Everyone who is no one will be there." He was a wit, Sol was.

Seducing with his perverse charm, backed by the atmosphere of the track, even the smell of the place – horses, beer, peanuts, urine and tobacco. The street of dreams. It was a vice. Something for nothing. And it didn't hurt knowing how disgusted my parents would be if they knew I was going to the track. They hated gambling, particularly my father, the high-minded, Dr. Brucher. Thrills and spills. My new bailiwick.

The first time we go, Sol picks us up, Mac and me, in his beat up '59 Volkswagen Bug. We make the trip in eight minutes. Yonkers. There's something about the blackness of the place at night, how it's lit up as the pacers and trotters take their warm-ups. We pay our two buck entry fees and get our fifty cent programs ten minutes before the first race, plunk down our two dollar minimums on the Daily Double 1 and 4.

Sure as you are born, that 1 horse comes in first by four lengths. The second race is much tighter. The 4 is in the thick of a three-way photo finish that goes to the judges for a decision. Mac and I both bet the 1–4. So we wait and overhear other equally expectant fans yelling loudly, "Put 'em up there." "Put 'em up there."

Finally, the parimutuel board flashes, the winner.... 4. Mac and I, jumping and screaming. The board shows a $22.80 payoff for the daily double. Beaming, the two of us run to the cashier's window to collect. And we're on our way.

Two days later, still under Sol's mentorship, we win another daily double. This time the payoff, one hundred dollars, only serves to plant the spike of addiction. It marks the beginning of what for Mac, Mark and me becomes a three times a week habit that lasts through our senior year in high school. And all this under the expert tutelage of our arch degenerate guide, Sol Danceway, "The King of Yonkas."

CHAPTER 8

Arnie Alone

A year and a half later, the beginning of tenth grade, 1965, this is the shape my life takes. Less and less interest in school. Doing the minimum in Geometry, Biology and Spanish, while reading excessively in English and History. I read history books, assigned and unassigned. Another love, reading Steinbeck and Hemingway for English is also consuming. With my now best friends, Mac and Mark, harness racing and poker are core parts of our modus vivendi. Communication with my parents is more and more reduced, my mood around them often sullen, negative. My life more private and my goings on more secretive. At home, I am frequently short, blunt, but mostly repair to the sanctuary of my room. Living for my friends, the track, poker, old movies, basketball and singing rock 'n' roll. And girls.

Of course, the bulk of my thoughts revolve around the fairer sex, but I am still honing my Bogart/James Dean tough guy persona. I get pretty tongue-tied with girls, especially the pretty ones. I mean,

I'd made out with girls, mostly in seventh and eighth grades, and felt up a couple by ninth, but under all my developing bravado and invented coolness, my experience base with girls was pretty lean. And this is starting to bother me.

Of course, by the end of tenth grade, June '66, none of us has scored. The three of us decide we have to solve this, our common problem, once and for all. So, Mark and I decide to take action. We forge a pact that we will get laid by the end of the summer after tenth grade or die. A dramatic gesture signaling the intensity of our ardor and our desperation.

On a muggy June night after school is out for the summer, we hop on the train to Grand Central, take the shuttle to Times Square and then take the IRT subway to The West Village. We hear there is a burgeoning hippie scene there. Marijuana, LSD, psychedelic music, weird clothes, long hair and most importantly, FREE LOVE.

Word from older guys in high school was—"All you gotta do is go down to 4th street around MacDougal, the heart of The Village, and just hang out. You don't have to do anything and you'll get laid. They come to you."

How stupid can you be? Well, pretty stupid. Mark and I land on MacDougal near the Café Au Go and Café Wa. We lean against brick walls for the better part of an hour, smoking Viceroys, waiting for something to happen. Guess what? We get approached several times. Various street hustlers (males) looking to sell us pot or LSD. But not once does a "hippie chick," as we call them, even come close. Damn it. We look at each other after forty five minutes of this idiocy and Mark says to me, “We’re pathetic.”

Me: ”You’ve got that right, pal. We’re never gonna get laid and that’s all there is to it.”

With our heads down, we walk into the Café Wa, where Jimmy James and the Flames and the Immortal Blue Flame, a psychedelic band is playing. This guy, Blue Flame, plays with his teeth. Black guy. Astounding. A few months later, we find out he has changed his name back to Jimi Hendrix, his real name, and by June of next year he’s a superstar with his appearance at the Monterey Pop Festival.

Way too humiliated to go home, in complete defeat, we hole up in Grand Central Station around midnight, sleep in phone booths or scrunching down in the back seat of a rotating new white Ford Mustang on display in the mezzanine. Somehow, we manage to avoid being rousted by the cops, arriving home irritable and bleary-eyed around sunrise, having done that Village thing, man. What a fucking joke.

CHAPTER 9

Girls/Boys on Girls

I'm telling you, we didn't have a clue. Back in New Rochelle that summer, confronted with the same dilemma. *Meeting chicks*. How to get them to like us and get them to want to sleep with us without appearing too obvious or predatory. Mark and I think we've found the perfect venue, getting jobs on the Long Island Sound in a beach club. We are hired at a dollar an hour to clean cabanas and hand out lounge chair cushions to the patrons and generally make ourselves available and useful to the members as needed. Basically, the job gave us ample opportunity to ogle girls in bikinis. A mixed blessing, constant stimulation with no ability to do anything about it.

Mark, frustrated with my sadistic prodding, daring him to smoke, broke down eventually and began smoking Marlboros. I was already a pack a day Marlboro man. After two weeks on the job, with the summer heat, bikini allure, blocked channels of expression and ongoing boredom, Mark is soon perusing the Riviera Beach Club lawn in search for discarded, unsmoked cigarette butts. For some reason, I love the sadistic power I feel I exercise over Mark's not-so-secret cravings. Probably similar to the sick delight a pusher gets when he hooks a new user on heroin. Sick enjoyment.

Nights, we drink, go to beach club dances, eventually ending up at pizzerias or all night diners. NO TAKERS. We had nothing. No rap, no finesse. What do you say after hello? How to not telegraph our horn-dog desires? It's a problem. Pitifully, night after night, searching and not finding, drinking with the boys and then heading home in frustration. The girls we know from school and the neighborhood, the ones we've grown up with, we write off as either stuck up or prudes. I wonder what they think of us. Hard to tell.

My guess from what a platonic friend, Sue, tells me is that we are seen as alternately oafy, stuck up, barbaric or hopelessly childish. Great. The gulf between us and them feels huge and insurmountable.

A consolation, the music that summer is great. All the local garage bands play lots of Mitch Ryder – "Little Latin Lupe Lu," Wilson Pickett/the Young Rascals – "Midnight Hour," and Paul Revere and the Raiders- "Just Like Me." Songs with easy simple chord changes. Every band has these three songs in their repertoire. "Wild Thing" by the Trogs is also prominently featured. On the other hand, nothing but ogling was the bill of fare that summer and into the fall.

One night in October, the three of us, Mark, Mac and me, head out to the track and hit a $200 Daily Double. My parents are out of town that weekend visiting my older brother Dave, now a junior at the University of Wisconsin. So, I have the run of the house.

It's Columbus Day weekend. The height of autumn leaves. Indian Summer. Leaves- crimson, gold and yellow and crunchy.

Friday night, ecstatic from our track winnings and feeling super, Mac informs us of a gathering happening at Lorna Guttman's house, a tenth grader. Being juniors, Mac figures we can get in. Mark bows out. He often does, mysteriously, when it comes to going to parties or girls' houses. He likes dances or going to the city, but for some reason when it comes to smaller gatherings, he bails. Mac, on the other hand is always ready. Ready for anything, really.

So, feeling "very cool" we make it to Lorna's to sample the tenth grade wares. We're greeted at the door by Lorna's younger sister, Fran, a fox in her own right, who tersely informs us Lorna and her "friends" are downstairs, "in case we cared."

Sauntering down the stairs with our most self-assured, casual lope, borrowed from our observation of older Blacks we'd seen at the track, Mac immediately goes for the pretzels and beer. Lorna's parents are out of town, too, so no parental uptight vibes. I sit on the couch and notice a brunette who looks familiar sitting on a stationary bike. Wearing straight legged jeans, brown turtleneck sweater with unfashionably curly hair, she sports a smattering of freckles. I glance over at her. She looks back, smiles and cackles nervously. A grin appears on my face straight out of Paul Newman in "Hud," when he tries to seduce Patricia Neal. A shit-eating grin I believe you call it. We start to talk. Believe it or not folks, this was not my forte. But on this night, for some reason, the words are flowing. Feeling relaxed and, for a change, very confident. I'm sure the track winnings are making a difference. I'm acting like schmoozing is no big deal. Do it all the time.

You know what? She seems to be responding, too. Laughing at my jokes. The banter is alive. Turns out, this Marla is practically my next door neighbor. Lives two streets away and used to ride the same bus together to junior high. Not that I noticed. On top of that, she is the best girl athlete in her grade in sixth grade. We went to the same elementary school. God, the difference of a few years. What a bod on her! She is awesome. Great curves, bod, a fox overnight. We talk for an hour non-stop. Easiest conversation I ever had with a female who wasn't my mother, with the exception of my brother's girlfriend, Louise.

As the clock heads towards midnight, Mac and I catch each other's eye and silently bid our adieus. He to Lorna, me to Marla Mascowitz, the girl, and bound up the stairs of their basement and drive home. That night on the tube, William Holden and Kim Novak in "Picnic" enthralls and engrosses me. Teary-eyed as I watch, identifying with the Holden character who is playing a thirty-five-year-old loser wanderer, making his last stand for love, another part of my mind-plotted strategy. I decide Marla Mascowitz would be mine. I know it in a place I hadn't felt in my gut since my halcyon days on the diamond and gridiron. Not for a while.

The next day, Saturday, New Rochelle is playing Mt. Vernon at McKenna Field in New Rochelle. Around 10:00 a.m., I hop into my Ford Falcon and swing by Marla's, stop on a dime at the curb, try to walk patiently to her front door, only mildly nervous. Alicia,

Marla's mother, who's an attractive, pleasant sounding woman with a southern accent, greets me. Pleased that a gentleman caller is here to see her daughter, she invites me into the living room while hollering for Marla to come down from her bedroom upstairs.

Almost immediately, Marla bounces down the stairs, delighted. In my usual diplomatic manner, I blurt out, "Do you want to go to the football game with me today? We're playing Mt. Vernon."

To my shock, she says, "Sure, that'd be great."

"Cool," says I. "I'll be back at noon to get you, okay?"

"Great," she beams excitedly.

And two hours later I go to get her, and we're off in my Falcon. Damn, this is easy. This girl really likes me. She's easy to talk to. Likes to laugh. We have things to talk about. Football, gossip about teachers, who's going out with who. Amazing. There's this relaxation here. I can't explain. There's that other feeling there, too. Horn dog alley. But that one's much more familiar and ever-present.

New Rochelle whips Mt. Vernon, 27-10. At Antonio's Pizza Parlor after the game, a momentary glumness takes me over as I recall the post-mortem tennis match conversation with my father from three years ago. But I quickly shake it off. I'm with Marla now. And this is today. And I'm happy to be here. In fact, it feels great to be here with her. Fun, excited and relaxed. Alive. We split three slices and two cokes then drive back to the north end of town where we live, taking the slow route down Pinebrook Lake. Dusk, around 4:30.

In the car, with the ubiquitous AM radio, "Devil With the Blue Dress" plays, soon to be our anthem, maybe because it's playing on this first date. Maybe because it encapsulates the feeling of being together. This song is followed by The Association's "Cherish" and The Four Tops' "Reach Out." Then switching over to the FM dial, to WOR-FM, an underground rock station, new to radio, a new creation, in fact, a song I vaguely know but like comes on:

In the chilly hours and minutes
Of uncertainty, I want to be
In the warm hold of your loving mind

To feel you all around me
And to take your hand along the sand
Ah, but I may as well try and catch the wind

Moved by the mood of the song and the aptness of sentiment conveying the tenderness of the moment, my head turns tentatively towards Marla, sitting two inches from me. We kiss. Short, on the lips, only to be followed by a longer more passionate kiss. Instinctively, I stop the car along the road and soon we're in a tight clinch, going at it – *Making Out.*

Speechless, excited, yet somehow easy. Natural. After an eternity or less, we break apart and avert our eyes. Embarrassed or shy, maybe frightened by the power of the attraction and our ardor, we exchange a bemused glance, looking away but holding hands the rest of the way home. Not really talking.

As the car stops at Marla's house and I open the car door for her, she takes two steps towards the house and then turns around and in a clear sweet voice at half-yell level I hear, "Arnie, I like you. I want to see you again." Stunned, I reply, "Okay," with a half-smile, not really able to muster any more words.

A short wave of the fingers with my right hand, and I watch her spiritedly sprint into her house. Back in my car, I u-turn and am home in half a minute. Feelings, feelings I have never felt before. Light-headed, yet clear. Warm and cozy. I open my front door and race to the kitchen refrigerator. There, I take out three pieces of gefilte fish, inhale them and head upstairs for a three hour nap. When I wake up, my first thought is: I have a girlfriend! Thank you, world.

CHAPTER 10

Marla Mascowitz
The Case Mase

I don't know what it is. He's a wild man. Me, a nice suburban Jewish girl, shy, giggling too much, a total tomboy just a couple of years ago. All about climbing and playing ball. I can't get enough of it, especially with the boys. And I am a pretty good hitter, too. Girls are okay, but I like hanging out with boys more.

And boys, not the shrinking violet types, I like the rough and ready ones more. Still and all, I am still pretty shy. But when my shape changed, I don't know what happened. All of a sudden, so self-conscious. Giggly and awkward. I blush for no reason at all. My friends Becky and Lorna are a bit more outgoing. Easier and more relaxed with the boys. We are all pretty good students. Love to dance, especially to soul music. Our parents are all pretty okay, I guess. Get us nice clothes and stuff, send us to nice sleep-away camps and all.

I sort of knew Arnie for a long time. We went to junior high on the same bus for a couple of years. I'd see him with his parents at the Chinese restaurant, Sunday nights. He seemed okay. Friendly, sort of cute. A good athlete. More than just good. Always carried a glove with him and always wore sneakers. Had a rep for being one of the best athletes in the school. But don't think I ever had more than a two second conversation with him before that night at Lorna's.

That day, I am tired from shopping with Mom. But Lorna encourages me, "Come on, maybe some older boys will be there." We'd done this, Lorna, Becky and me, a few times since the beginning of ninth grade. I am beginning to think I'll never meet anyone. Lorna and Becky have had a few make out- feel up sessions in the last year or so ("second base" as we say). But we are known in the circuit by the boys as being prudish. I never felt that way about myself. There just hadn't been much opportunity. Or I hadn't met a boy I really liked that much.

My parents, especially my mom, raised me to be treated with respect. And I just don't like boys who are rude, nasty or stupid. Of course, it helps if they aren't too shy. I am already too shy. So the boy needs to take the lead a little. Lorna and Becky are more outgoing. They don't worry so much about who takes the lead. They both like quieter boys anyway. With me, a sense of humor helps.

That night, it's October, I am a little under the weather. Kind of tired and low key, if you know what I mean, but as soon as he walks in, I can feel the electricity. As soon as I see him with his swagger, in his chestnut suede jacket with the rips, and his white tee shirt, little shock waves are in the air as if we are both caught up in a magnetic force field. It's intense. Nervous and smiling all at once. Surges of something sweep me up as our eyes meet. But I keep pedaling on the stationary bike, trying not to look flustered. But also trying not to act unfriendly. He approaches me after a while, bobbing his head to the Temptations. He comes up to me.

Arnie: "Don't I know you?"

Me: "Of course. I'm Marla Mascowitz. We're neighbors. We rode the same bus together for years. To Albert Leonard. "

Arnie: "I remember you now. You were a great baseball player. Best girl ballplayer at Davis. The best in your grade."

Me: "Thanks," beaming. "I hear you're pretty good, too."

Arnie: "Used to be. I took two years off, eighth and ninth grades. It hurt my timing. My hitting and fielding both have suffered. Trying to play catch up now. It's the story of my life. It's hard but I'm gettin' there. You like the Temptations I see."

Me: "The best. I especially like the Motown groups, you know, Smokey, The Tops. How 'bout you?"

Arnie: "Yeah, I like it all," cooly, breezily. "You're pretty."

And I'm floored. "Thanks, you're pretty cute yourself," I blurt out.

"Damn, you're not the same Marla Mascowitz I used to see on that damn bus. You're, you're so grown up."

"Ah, you just haven't seen me in a while," I say.

"Looking good," Arnie says.

"How well do you know Lorna and Becky?" I was trying to change the subject.

"I know Mac, and Mac knows everybody. I came with Mac. You know Mac?" he asks.

"Yeah," I say. "Isn't he the guy they call 'primitive man'?"

"Yeah, that's him." Arnie says. "Wild man, I guess I am, too."

Me: "That's what I hear."

Arnie: "Don't believe everything you hear."

Me: "Yeah, reps are made and lost on rumors."

Arnie: "Yeah."

Me: "What's the word on me?"

Arnie, hesitating: "Ah, you know, nice girl, good athlete."

Me: "That's not what I mean."

Arnie, smiling: "What do you mean?"

Me: "If you don't know, maybe you'll have to find out."

Arnie, taken aback: "Um, what do you mean?"

Me: "You'll have to figure it out, I guess."

Arnie: "Oh, that stuff. You mean that *REP* stuff. Oh!"

Me: "Yeah, that stuff. So, what's my rep?"

Arnie: "I can't say. But it's definitely good news."

Me: "For who?"

Arnie: "I can't say."

Me, good naturedly: "You're a drip, Arnie."

Arnie: "Haven't been called that in a while. Maybe since sixth grade. That's a blast from the past."

Just then, Mac yells over to Arnie, saying he has to split or he is gonna be in trouble. So, that's the end of our conversation and first real meeting. I remember Arnie says goodbye with a shy but warm cheshire cat smile. Then Mac bounces over, introduces himself again, and whispers something into Arnie's ear. Then Arnie says to me, "Great talking to you. Maybe I'll see you again."

CHAPTER 11

The First Few Dates (Marla's Version)

The thing of it is – he is just so cool. Really nice with my mother, gentlemanly and courteous. She takes to him right away. Dad, too. Only Dad is a bit more reserved, less enthusiastic. But that is Dad's nature. As for me, I am just so thrilled. He comes over that next day. Total surprise. Hint of how it will be. Unpredictable. Never know what will happen next. A thrill a minute. I really like him. I mean, as a person and I am really attracted.

We also have one bad thing in common – we both smoke Marlboros. So, when he takes me to the Mt. Vernon game that day, he doesn't make a big deal of it when I take out a cigarette. He's a pack and a half a day man himself. His driving is a little strange. Kind of aggressive, kind of fast one minute, then the next minute he's going below the speed limit, as though he isn't paying attention. I don't mind though, that much. It just feels so comfortable *and* exciting.

The football game is great. We win big. Everyone is there. Lorna, Becky and the whole north end of New Rochelle crowd. Some of Arnie's friends, too, who I don't know. It's like the world is opening up. I can't stop giggling.

Then, we take the slow way home. One of those beautiful crisp fall days, orange, red and green leaves that look and smell perfect. He takes me by the lake and then that great song comes on. You know that Donovan song that the Blues Project does "Catch the Wind." Next thing, we're kissing and making out. It's so out of sight. There's only one problem. I really like him and my parents just told me yesterday that we're moving to Chicago because my Dad got a better job. I hate it. Just when I finally meet someone. Well, if I have to go, I'm gonna have some fun. I'm gonna let Arnie get to third base with me. I'll probably never see him again. And I need to find out what all the fuss is about.

CHAPTER 12

One Week Later

A week later, Lorna's parents are out again. This time I don't have to crash Lorna's house with Mac. Lorna and Marla invite me to come over. Lorna, by this time, has a new boyfriend, Ronnie M., an old poker buddy friend from the "Skip" game. Word on the street is Marla is leaving town after Christmas and she's hot to trot.

Gonna let me go to third base with her. Ronnie and I drive to Lorna's house, the one with the stationary bike in the basement. I am overflowing with anticipation. We are not disappointed. After we have beers, he goes with Lorna to one bedroom and I go with Marla to another.

Like rabbits, we must be going at it for two hours. Intense. Second base right away. What a bod. Must have been 36C or something. Not being standoffish. Spending time isn't boring either. We have a good time hanging out, too. Marla loves that soul music. Me, too. And she is very playful and physical – love taps on the arm, a lot – and actually punches. It's cool. It feels great to have a girlfriend. Cute and fun. Me and my friends quickly give her a nickname, "The Case Mase." "Case" being one of our slang expressions for "whole." Like a case dollar. Or "case ace" – solid. The "CASE MASE": a good one to have around. Ronnie and Lorna are doing their thing, too. Don't come up for air for a couple of hours either. The four of us get together afterwards- battered, bruised and tussled. The most fun I ever had as a teenager. I swear.

CHAPTER 13

Arnie on Marla / Marla on Arnie

Arnie

I must have lucked out because Marla is ready. We make out about forty times in the next few months. Marla, figuring she's out of here, so she's gonna have a good time and I am her candidate. So, she lets me go to second and third base, further than I had ever gone with a girl and further than she had ever gone. Plus, we have a lot of fun. Dancing, going to the track, going to Nathan's. There is only one thing wrong with her that I can see. She isn't the most intellectual or aware person I'd ever met and I can get bored pretty quickly. But, what the hell, I figure, she likes me a lot. Actually, I think she loves me and I find myself growing attached to her. I also like the idea of having a girlfriend.

It does wonders for my head and status in my scene. Marla is highly regarded. Popular, everyone thinks she is fun, neat or groovy.

Of course, with all this good stuff, I take her for granted. Never call her. Could be inconsiderate and I have this bad tendency of flirting with her girlfriends, flirtatious, cute and well-built in their own right. Always restless, I guess. Never content. Grass is greener bullshit. I don't know.

Anyway, I guess we're going steady. Then around X-Mas, Marla finds out her family is not going to move to Chicago as originally planned. That changes things. She tightens up around me in our make out sessions. Less loose, not so wild. She becomes cautious all of a sudden, worries about whether I respect her, what her parents might think and not wanting to get a bad rep. We revert to dry humping. The well is dry. I get frustrated.

Being a virgin and all, I get blue balls regularly. I also am increasingly interested in other girls. Especially Becky, one of Marla's best friends. I finally get Becky's consent to go out with me after two weeks of haggling, negotiating, imploring and multiple mind-changes on her part. The situation is getting complicated.

Marla

These last three months with Arnie have been so great. I guess I lead him on a bit though. I figure I am leaving and so might have given the impression that I was gearing up to go all the way. We get to third base, which I let him do, which I must admit was pretty exciting and scary. New for me. But when I find out we aren't moving, something changes inside of me. I begin to get scared and worried. All of a sudden things get serious. I realize I like Arnie a lot and I am worried I will lose him. So I cut off his advances. Piss him off. But I don't want to be treated like a slut.

Plus, I'm never sure how he feels about me. He never tells me. During Christmas break, I tell Arnie I love him for the first time. He looks pleased and worried at the same time but he immediately changes the subject. It seems the more I say that stuff to him the more he stays away. Arnie can be a real prick sometimes. Inconsiderate, rude and crude. Always commenting on other girls. I hate that. It makes me jealous and insecure. But we are close nevertheless. I really love the excitement of being around him. He is unpredictable. Always keeps me guessing. It is great. Sort of.

CHAPTER 14

Trouble at School

I don't want to create the wrong impression here. Just because I have a real girlfriend for the first time in my life doesn't mean everything is hunky dory. School, which had always been problematic for me, is at crisis proportions by now, my junior year, at least, if you believe my parents' reactions to my academics. Actually not much has changed in four of my five subjects. A's and B's in English and History, B's and C's in Math and Science. But Spanish, you can forget about that.

Spanish III is my first period class at 7:30 a.m. on the heels of a Spanish II teacher last year who gave everyone at least a B just for showing up. Well, those chickens are coming home to roost. My Spanish III teacher assumes, as she should, I guess, that everyone in the class is capable of doing Spanish III work. She takes for granted that we all have proficiency in the material covered the previous year. Nice work, if you can get it. By week two, I realize that I am in way over my head. Not particularly liking the teacher and not thinking for one minute that I should approach the teacher or my parents with my dilemma (more Bogey here), I just let it ride. Actually, I do more than just let it ride. My weekly attendance averages about three out of five classes. The rest of the time, me and some buddies can be seen at the local deli during first period reading the local racing sheet, handicapping the evening's races.

Avoid, deny, pretend all is well. That's the mode. It doesn't really work. November, one afternoon, I come home from school to a scene I am unaccustomed to seeing. There at the kitchen table with her hands covering her face, sits my mother wiping away tears.

"I just got a call from Miss Mossi, your Spanish teacher. She says your attendance is minimal and you're flunking Spanish. Where have you been? I don't know what I'm gonna do with you. What did I do wrong? I thought I was a good parent. Tell me where did I go wrong?"

"Ma, I'll do better, I promise," upset that my mother is upset and wanting desperately to make it right.

"Do you need help? I don't mean just school. You seem so secretive, quiet and sullen all the time. Is something wrong?"

"No ma," I say. "I'm just not trying hard enough. The teacher is boring. But I will, I promise."

The conversation is excruciating. I hate to see my mother sad and disappointed with me. It really matters to me what she thinks far more than what my father thinks. Our conversation leaves me feeling really shitty. With pangs of guilt I hadn't experienced since the first time I lost $100 at the track and didn't even have a quarter for the ritual track exit pretzel. I vow to do better. I can't stand feeling like a loser.

When my father gets wind of the Spanish disaster, he is concerned and pissed. He grounds me from going out for two weeks. As is his wont, he tries grilling me on my attitude, study habits, friends, values, etc. etc. to see if he can come up with an answer to his middle son's problems. I perplex him. Dave, my older brother, is launched, basically. A junior at Wisconsin, straight A's and a History major. Lew, the baby, now in seventh grade, is also a pleasure. Straight A's. He'd already skipped second grade. Never a problem. Cheerful, popular, good athlete. But, me, I'm a pain in the ass, is all I am. That's what my father usually thinks but now he is saying these things out loud.

"You'll end up at 'Frank and Cedar's,' that's where you'll go to college if you don't buckle down," he would say sarcastically, alluding to my becoming a clerk at the discount retail clothing store in Philadelphia where he grew up.

"You want to be a bum, then you'll be a bum. I don't know where you get your friends. And worst of all, your attitude stinks. You'd better change it, brother, or it's gonna be your funeral."

His lectures are very enlightening as you can imagine. Not too motivating. They succeed in activating my guilt. Especially my guilt at my parents' disappointment, particularly my mother's which makes me want to do better. My father's lecturing and low level tirades makes me feel like he could care less about me or my feelings. It seems all he cares about is results, grades – success. Fuck him, I think. I'll do what I want.

So there it is. Feeling bad for my mother, pissed at my old man, who I think is only interested in how my performance reflects on him. Not really motivating. It doesn't make for my being a happy camper at home. Mostly back and forth between anger, resentment and guilt.

CHAPTER 15

Psych Testing and the Man of La Mancha

So Mom and Dad decide I need to be evaluated. Something is dreadfully wrong with this boy and they have to get to the bottom of it and find out what it is right away. So to the NYU Center for Psychological Testing I go. There, for the next four weeks, I am treated to a battery of testing instruments designed to ferret out what is happening to me. They administer a variety of personality, intelligence and vocational tests designed to figure me out.

Upon completion of the evaluation, there's a debriefing meeting that my parents and I attend with a Dr. White, the psychologist evaluator. Dr. White's a stern man. While imparting the results, he looks straight into my eyes and announces with some stridency that I am an angry, sullen young man, lacking in discipline, along with poor study habits, in desperate need of psychological help before it is too late.

He didn't elaborate on the "too late," only suggesting firmly that I need twice weekly psychotherapy. Surprised and somewhat numb on the surface, I am strangely agreeable. I nod my willingness and openness to the idea and once again pledge to try harder and do better. The whole ritual with my parents is repetitive, hollow, meaningless. I know my momentary sincerity and genuineness will never last. I believe the comments my parents are making about me, despite trying not to, and begin to entertain doubts as to whether I can or will be anything but a loser. Maybe they are right. Maybe I am stuck.

Ah, I'd said that hopeful stuff before and it worked for a while. Both sides seem problematic to me, caring and not caring. Not caring leads to apathy, anger and envy of others, couched in criticism of others' phoniness. Caring leads to fears that I don't have what it takes to succeed. I secretly fear I lack the perseverance, confidence, ambition or energy. It seems hopeless yet I will try. I keep all of this to myself, of course. I keep my own council.

But glimpses of my dilemma come out the night my parents and I attend the new musical "Man of La Mancha," Don Quixote musicalized. After the play, dad does his usual probing interrogation about what I think. Not content with my usual one word answers, he provokes a response by attacking me on my study habits- a constant these days.

Unable to resist the bait, I finally reply, "I think the play was stupid. I thought it stunk. I thought the play was about the futility of idealism. Nobody cared. Where'd it get you? People will just laugh at you." Well, that really steams dad. He rails nonstop for a full ten minutes about my defeatist attitude.

Not a pretty picture. I feel bad, angry, frustrated and depressed all at the same time. The bulk of the ride home is spent in silence. Standard mode for the Brucher's these days. Please them, don't please them. No win either way. Finally at home, I pull the sheets over my head and go to sleep, not looking forward to the same old, same old when I wake up in the morning. At least, I have my friends and Marla. Oh yeah.

I temporarily forget about that good stuff when I get caught up in the hassles with my parents. "Thank God," I think when Mac wakes me up by calling me the next day. It's time to go back to The Village. He informs me that we will be going back to The West Village to see the new "underground" rock acts there. Yeah.

CHAPTER 16

Café Au Go

The Blues Project, Richie Havens, Judy Collins, damn, it beats the hell out of being with my stupid fucking parents, that's for sure. For our Village foray, we grab the train, Mark, Mac and me, at the Scarsdale station. Mac's dad is a big shot at a major music label that's producing these acts. They're part of the burgeoning folk-blues-rock scene rising out of the Dylan-influenced Village revival which is now escalating due to the huge popularity of the Beatles and Stones. The British Invasion. All of this is taking over the rock 'n' roll world and infecting the formerly "pure" folk and blues scene down there.

We're ripe for it. Mac has the most sophisticated musical taste of the three of us. He turns us on first to Dylan then Odetta, Buffy Saint Marie, Tim Harden, Tom Paxton. The folkie and blues scene. Mark and I are more soul, top 40 types. Beatles, Motown, pretty mainstream. But we we're fans who pride ourselves on our highly developed aesthetic tastes in music. We'd already been to some concerts. The Four Seasons, The Four Tops, Smokey and the Miracles, The Lovin' Spoonful, The Beach Boys, Simon and Garfunkel. But this is our first journey together into hippie/beatnik land just to see music. We are stoked.

Mark and I haven't been to The Village since our unsuccessful effort six months earlier to get laid. We don't see much music that night, except for an hour of Jimi James, aka Jimi Hendrix. Too busy doing nothing, standing around, looking cool, having no conversations, smoking too many cigarettes, waiting for the hippie chicks to fall into our laps.

Ah, but this night, chicks were not on the agenda. Mac and I are already "happening" with girlfriends. Mark receives the occasional pimp job from me with dates from Marla's friends. He never seems that intent moving in on women the way Mac and I do. Our styles are different but it doesn't matter that much. Music, sports and girls. The track, cards, a little politics, movies. A little pot once in a while. This is what we have in common and what we care about. What we are "into."

New Rochelle can be boring. We are each other's salvation, the best parts of our youths and more enjoyable than being with the girls actually. We exist, in large part, to report to each other on what we do with girls, our goings on. Oh, yeah. Of course, none of us really know how to be with girls. We're just trying on attitudes, poses, sort of like hairstyles. But anyway, in that smoky club on MacDougall, down in the basement, that little hole, that night Richie Havens is singing "High Flying Bird," we are... happening.

The singing and strumming on his guitar is simple, yet affecting on an elemental level. Basic, primitive but to the point. In the middle of the song, Mac elbows me in the ribs, pointing to the table at our left. I look over and shrug.

"There he is," Mac whispers, raising his eyebrows in excited surprise.

I raise my eyebrows, as if to say, "So."

Finally, he whispers to me, "That's Bob Dylan."

Me, I'm like so cool, I say, "Who gives a fuck."

That man was God at this point for anyone who is in. However, I consider myself and am considered to be a rock 'n' roll reactionary. More into the 50's early rock 'n' roll that Murray the K introduced me to on his WINS radio program. The only songs by Dylan I am really familiar with are the 45's, "Like a Rolling Stone" and "Positively Fourth Street" where we are, incidentally.

People who are into Dylan talk about him like he is the prophet of the coming apocalypse, particularly guys two or three years older. The ones in college, intellectual lefty types. The artsy-fartsies. The Hippnoscenti. Me and my mates are a little after the fact with the "new vanguard" of what would become the "Movement" and "Counterculture." It is still a budding bud of roses and mostly in Berkeley, San Francisco, New York, some in Cambridge, maybe Madison, Wisconsin, LA and smidgeons elsewhere – this late '66 early '67. You can sense it down in The Village.

The shift in The Village from six months earlier to the scene in late '66 is huge. The place has an atmosphere, a feel, a mood of expectancy. A crisp, smoky smell. Earnest, intent, self-righteous, righteous. A feeling of more than just imminent political change, you know. Civil rights, the Vietnam protest movement is starting to heat up. There is that for sure but something else deeper is in the air, being assaulted, challenged, felt, lived. Drugs definitely have something to do with it. Pot, acid, yes. I mean, we can all feel it, hear it in the music and in the conversations, looks, dress. What looked fifty years later like youthful rebellion, whatever, feels much more like the world is really changing. I mean the structure of life. 1966. The media hasn't quite taken hold of the thing completely yet. There are scenes developing in the Haight in San Francisco and here in The West Village. A vibe as well. That smell of incense, patchouli and cannabis everywhere.

People with glazed eyes, everywhere that felt sense of something new in the air—inchoate. Hard to put your finger on. Hard to capture. The old categories don't work. Pundits and critics not yet able to bottle it. Yeah. Beatles respectful of it. Dylan announcing it in his most surrealistic poems, "Ballad of the Thin Man," "Desolation Row," "Visions of Johanna." The feeling, all in there and everywhere. This is what is happening. Not just in Dylan's mind but being chronicled by him. The Stones have a piece of it, too. Guts-sex-sweat. Flowers, '66, The Byrds, "I'll Feel a Whole lot Better," the Beatles, "Good Day Sunshine."

Stoned, Mac rolls a doobie between acts and the music plays. We go into the bathroom of the Au Go Go where we are joined by several people toking up. Acapulco Gold. It's my second time getting stoned. "Seasoned vets" by now. The pot adds crispness and vividness to the scenes particularly when the imagination, triggered by sensations, is heightened by the smell of patchouli and leaves me feeling pleasant and relaxed. Combine this with Marlboros and a little beer, it really allows for the groove to get buckled, tightened and horizontalized. Senses altered. Feeling senses opened. Analytical mind intermittently on overdrive or quelled in a corner while sounds, images, smells, and libido perk up. The inner judge is temporarily tied up in knots. Bound and gagged. Mark's hair a Yidro. Mac, looking like a young Eric Clapton or an Apache warrior, long sideburns, shoulder-length hair, moustache, shoulder-length hair.. Me, sideburns, hair starting to hit the shoulder. All of us spaced out, groovin' to the music and ambiance.

CHAPTER 17

Pot 101, August '65 The First Time

The humidity and suffocating heat of summertime in midtown New York City is like walking through a bed of molasses. Getting to the same place than in spring or fall requires ten times more energy. But I don't care. I am tired of being cooped up at home in my parents' den watching TV all day. Getting into lower Manhattan in that heat feels like a major accomplishment.

Now, walking through Times Square, I notice the girly shows and peep shows and they pique my curiosity. I look but don't try to enter, being underage and all. I'm only fifteen but my mind is on only one thing, sex. As I'm aimlessly perusing, a young white guy with a paunch suddenly approaches me.

"Hey, buddy," he hollers, all business like and all, "want a blowjob?"

Thinking that this guy is reading my mind as if on some cosmic wavelength for a brief instant I think, "This is my lucky day. My ship has come in." With swirls of gonadal excitement, I breathlessly reply, "Sure, where's the girl?" Then as quick as my excitement flares, hopes are dashed.

"No woman, me."

Staggered, I manage to muster a, "No, thanks." Prelude to my summer of homoeroticism.

On that same note, a month later, while traveling in the Soviet Union with my folks, we are coming out of the Bolshoi Ballet in Moscow. A grey and spectral rain, streets indistinguishable from one another. Street signs written in Greek/Aramaic. Told by my folks to cross the street to fetch a cab, turns out there's one catch. The crosswalk is underground. Once underground, I notice three exits, taking one, I come up out of the underground and can't see my parents. They should be on the other side of the street. I don't know where I am. Panicking, I start to walk and quickly become more lost.

I'm looking for Dad in his black raincoat, Mom in her grey and black-checkered coat, bundled up with her umbrella in hand. They are nowhere to be found. Heart pounding, starting to sweat. I'm lost. In my panic, I try chatting up anyone desperate to find someone who speaks English. No one stops, other than a few drunks, who recognize my American accent and yell, "CALIFORNIA, CALIFORNIA," as if, I don't know, I'm from there? They have relatives there? Or they're just thinking of Hollywood. I have no clue. Freaking out. I keep moving and getting more lost. After attempting to chat up another drunk, a voice appears off to my side in a white cape, green beret, and round shaped spectacles.

"I'll help you! I speak Russian and English."

I say, for some reason, "Are you Jewish?"

He replies, "I'm from Cairo, Egypt."

My eyes go up to the back of my head and I say to myself, "I'm doomed. What am I gonna do now?" By now, I'm teary eyed, frantic, thinking quickly I say, "Okay."

"Where are you from?" he asks and then "Where are you staying?"

"New York and the Peking Hotel," I mutter.

"Not sure where that is, but I'll inquire and get directions. Don't worry, I'll get you back to the hotel." He speaks with a vaguely English accent and I pick up a kind of effeminate vibe. He's friendly and comforting. I'm relieved and nervous at the same time. Pretty sure he's gay, although that's not the word I would have used back then. Back then it was, "I'm pretty sure this man is a faggot." My fear is confirmed minutes later when he sidles up to me as we walk, as if he's comforting me. My dilemma: lost and feeling dependent on this man for my safety and my getting back to the hotel. What should I do?

As we continue walking, he makes a move to hold my hand. Initially, I push away, but as we keep walking, he grows more persistent and I change tactics, deciding to let him. I need this guy and don't want to alienate him. So, I let him hold my hand. This is survival time. I'm a little nauseated by the whole thing but can't get around feeling like I need this guy. The more we walk and talk, the clearer it is that this guy wants to be with me but he also seems genuinely concerned for my safety. Finally, after about an hour of this, walking and asking people for directions, he finds the right bus to take me back to the hotel.

I'm relieved once we get on the bus, except the whole bus is filled with Chinese people from the People's Republic, my country's enemy at the time. I feel like I'm operating behind enemy lines somehow. The Egyptian guy riding with me on the bus makes his move. He says he would like to see me again. Like tomorrow.

I say, "Sure. That would be great. My parents would love to meet you and thank you."

Not mincing words, he says, "No, Arnie, that won't be necessary. But I would like to see you, just you."

I say, "Sure," knowing it won't happen.

We get to the lobby of the hotel where I'm staying and he says goodbye. I thank him profusely and tell him I will see him tomorrow. He repeats that he doesn't want to meet my folks to be thanked. That it's not necessary. And then he is gone.

I can only imagine what's going on with my parents. I'm sure they are beside themselves. And they are. My mother's head is outside the hotel window. She's queasy because she's sure I'm dead. My father is in action, on the phone to the U.S. embassy blasting at them to send the police to find me in a blistering, desperate, raging tone.

I'm downstairs now and go to the concierge who speaks English. He tells me my parents are looking for me and asks if I'm okay. I nod in response and head to the room as waves of panic and dread reemerge, but a different kind, a more familiar kind. Like the kind in anticipation of a tongue-lashing and a lecture that I'm used to. He's gonna be crazy, the old man. The old lady's gonna be chain smoking.

I knock on the door. Dad appears. Before anyone can say a word, I enter with my quick darting feet and mumble, "Don't hit me."

"Hit you? I just want to kiss you. Where have you been?" Dad bellows with obvious relief and glee. My mother turns around to hug me. Ashen, trembling and, yes, chain smoking. They're exhausted. I'm exhausted. My father, in celebration, gets out the bottle of Schnapps, the bitter drink of Jewish angst, and we all do a toast to survival and return to freedom.

We are never closer than that night or for that matter the rest of our trip. From Moscow, we head to Amsterdam, Paris and London. For the remainder of the two weeks, we communicate intimately. A month later, having returned from Europe, in late August, I smoke my first joint of Acapulco Gold. And that, as they say, was that.

CHAPTER 18

August '65 Pot / I Got You Babe

For Christ's sake, after these near misses, in Times Square and Moscow, I need to do something to prove my manhood – in the Humphrey Bogart-John Wayne sense. I am afraid I am Montgomery Clift, you know, the rumors about his being AC/DC. The truth was that the Bogart shtick is a lot of bravado, underneath I *am* really a lot more like Montgomery Clift. Soft, sensitive. By the same token, after the experience in Moscow my confidence surges. It is good to know I can survive in adverse circumstances, by hook or by crook. It turns out that it makes me feel a little more adventurous.

An opportunity arises less than a week after we get back to the States. Mark and I are informed by an acquaintance/ friend, "Fast Eddie Olderman," a kid who lives down the block, that he is looking to sell. Wonders if we are interested. Well, we are but also anxious about it. We agree to meet up just before sunset to try out the pot at

Davis, my old elementary school. When Mark and I show up, Eddie is already there. The place is empty. We congregate on the asphalt blacktopped baseball diamond at second base where he takes out the joints and we pass them around. We are all back to back to back as the joints are passed around as if facing the four winds, or in this case the three winds. Two joints are inhaled. No effect. Twenty minutes later, still no effect. Frustrated, Mark and I decide to walk, leaving Eddie at second base.

Now it's 9:30 and pitch black outside. As we walk across the blacktop, suddenly, there appears a sheet of wallpaper, three feet wide and high in front of my eyes. Checkerboard shaped with diamond and triangle-shaped designs and club and heart shaped-design figures on the bottom half of the squares. I'm seeing wallpaper. Feeling funny. Strange, weird, not unpleasant. Not drunk or speedy from my asthma spray. Something different. Mentally different. Hard to explain. We're moving slower, talking less, looking more, observing more, less emotional, and we're kind of more in sync. Less cerebral. We're walking in unison. Left foot first, then right. Breathing in unison. Wordless, yet in sync. Or so it seems.

I feel hyperaware. Continuing to walk in silence, breathing through our noses the thick, humid suburban air as we walk down Rogers Drive onto Waverly and through my neighbor's back yard into the backyard of my house. Whew, safe and sound and it feels good to be home, strangely enough. Slightly scary, being stoned. The outside world, the stars, louder and brighter than they should be, assuming a menacing quality. Yeah, it's good to be inside. Mark, meanwhile, has not said a word to me in over a half hour. Feels like forever. Just looks over on occasion, smiling and gesturing as he lights a Marlboro, spitting tobacco bits with his tongue. We're in worlds of our own, in silence but strangely intimate in close physical proximity.

Mark decides to sleep over as he "'aint goin' home in this condition." Just as well. We raid the refrigerator, which is filled with fried chicken, inhale its contents, everything but the bones. Mark chugs a bottle of Tab and I chug some Borden's milk. We're ready! Stoned munchies. It's Saturday night and my parents are out and off to see "My Fair Lady" in the movies for the second time. God, they're boring. I'm thinking, nothing much to do but turn on the radio. WOR-FM. Murray the K's new station. Calls himself the fifth Beatle. Now getting into Dylan, Donovan, the Byrds. The new underground FM radio scene. The Beach Boys come on and then a song I haven't heard before because I was in Europe the past five weeks sightseeing. It's kind of hokey, with a driving beat, the lyrics very much about young love today. Rebellious in its way. "I Got You Babe," by Sonny and Cher. It speaks to me in a weird heartfelt way.

Mark and I look at each other, nodding approval and then speaking, agreeing that in the last month the music has really changed a lot on the radio since the Byrds' "Mr. Tambourine Man," and Dylan's "Like a Rolling Stone."

Mark says, "Amazing stuff."

Me: "I wonder what the Beatles are gonna do next? Yeah, and the Stones, what are they gonna do to follow up on 'Satisfaction?'" The

Beatles just performed at Shea Stadium that summer and Dylan was booed at the Newport Folk Festival and Forest Hills for turning electric.

It's quite a pleasant night, that first time on pot. By the time my parents come home from the Pix Theatre in White Plains, Mark and I are nodded out. Mark on the floor, me in bed. My mom throws a blanket over him and gets him a pillow as my dad announces through his yawn to my mom, "I'm hitting the hay. These guys are dead to the world."

Next day, we awake to another sunny, humid, muggy ninety degree day. We get stoned again, a pattern which continues on a biweekly basis for the next eighteen months. By the time my parents freak out and send me to the psychologist at N.Y.U. for evaluation, they have no clue that I am smoking dope and cigarettes for a year. They think I am "straight." They also don't know I drink with my buds regularly on weekends and in bars, or that I play poker on a regular basis, or that I frequently steal money out of my father's Donald Duck coin bank, known as "hitting the duck" to my friends. I use the quarters to go to the track, play poker or pool. They are mostly operating under a false impression. They really think I am basically a good kid, on the up and up but who is lazy and doesn't want to apply himself. Finally, October 1966, after four years of neglecting my schoolwork, behaving secretively and being withdrawn towards them, the jig is up. My parents conclude that I need help.

The 38 I get that first quarter in Spanish III is the clincher. My father finds out about the cards and the track and makes me feel bad about it. Didn't know where I get those ideas about life, or friends or interests. His constant comment is that, "It leads to nothing."

"Thanks, Dad," is my inevitable reply to this stuff. Sometimes, I say sarcastically, "Thanks, Dad, that was helpful." I really think the guy is a prick a lot of the time, not on my side. Anyways, they'd finally had enough of my act after that 38 in Spanish. So, that's what leads up to the psych eval and follow up visit to the shrink.

CHAPTER 19

It's Getting Better All the Time

The door of a hickory smoked-filled office in Scarsdale opens after my mother and I ring the brass door ringer. Dr. Chidas lets us into his office where we sit down on his schleppy gray couch, pretty funky by Scarsdale standards. This guy, a pipe smoker, rolly polly, thirty-five, tweed sports jacket, sense of humor, easy manner. I like him. Mom does, too. I love how his pipe smells. I can't smoke in his office. Actually, I don't ask if I can. After my mom leaves, we talk about my parents. Mom only stays ten minutes. I talk about my father a lot. I talk about Dave, my older brother, the goody two shoes, my grades, cigarette habit, booze, Marla. The important topics, I guess.

After I leave the first time, I feel better. Like I got a load off my mind. It is set up that I will see Chidas twice a week, Tuesdays and Thursdays after school so I won't have to miss baseball practice. It's one of the remaining "straight" activities I still care about. Center field. Second string. I should have been starting but my lack of hustle, discipline, my smoking and poor training regimen keeps my formerly superb game stagnant. I gave up "winning" after my traumatic tennis match with Ricky back in '63 so it becomes my excuse for not working on any sport for the last three and a half years. Except for "messing around." No dedication here, folks.

Yeah, that's what I do. I mess around. Sports, school, piano, acting. I don't really follow through on anything I claim I love. Claim I don't care, don't give a shit. Same excuse, pathetic, I'm pathetic – that's how I feel. I start opening up to Chidas about all of this, and the more I do, the better I feel.

I also begin to realize that I sure have a lot of problems. Actually, more than I ever knew. I begin to see in my own seventeen-year-old way how little confidence in myself I actually have. But I begin to see that I am of some value to myself.

Introspecting becomes an interpersonal affair. I don't have to ruminate or brood alone anymore. It begins to show quickly and immediately. My grades pick up from B's, C's and D's, I go to four B's and 1 D. The D is in Spanish. My average goes from 77 to 86 in one quarter which is my best since seventh grade. Dad and Mom, as you can imagine, are ecstatic. Mom more than Dad. Dad is wary of that D in Spanish and worries aloud.

Chidas meets with Dad, Mom, my younger brother Lew, now twelve, for family sessions. Chidas basically tells my dad to cool it a bit on the pressure and criticism, basically, to get off my back. Nice work, if you can get it. Dad tries and it lasts a couple of days but he can't contain his sarcasm or teasing tendencies. The man has high expectations and trouble knowing where he leaves off and where his kids begin.

Dad, in case you haven't figured this out, is not good for my ego these days. Mom is kind of helpless, supportive and nice. She gets a bang out of my academic improvement and expresses her pleasure with it. She likes Marla, too. Dad likes Marla also. The parents even start to like my friends better than before – Mac and Mark, that is. They always liked Ricky, my tennis rival, but Mac and Mark are of a rougher cut. Diamonds in the rough types. So, things are starting to look up, except for that damn Spanish. But this is the only quarter I pass Spanish. By the time finals come around, the Regents Exam in New York State, I need to get an 85 on it in order to pass the course. If I don't get at least that, it means summer school for me.

So by April, while celebrating an almost 10 point increase in my other courses, and even some improvement in Spanish, Dad says, "It looks like you'll be going to summer school." I even try keeping the grade from him. Even thought of changing the computer grade. A friend is changing grades for kids with a computer typewriter just like they use at school. I am flunking Spanish and am tempted to pay him the money to make it look like I am passing just to get the old man off my back. But somehow I know this is a losing strategy.

CHAPTER 20

May–June 67 Spanish

That spring, my father fixates on my failing grade in Spanish. While briefly noting my improvement in Math 11, Chemistry, English 11 and American History, especially Chemistry and Trigonometry, he quickly goes back to the F (60) numerical average that is mine at the three-quarter mark of the academic year. With a look of consternation, pursed lips and menacing determination, his veiled disapproval begins to speak.

"You must pass Spanish. It is not acceptable for you to go to summer school. It will screw up mom's and my summer plans, which you will not do. Therefore, here is what will be done. Beginning tomorrow and every morning for the next six weeks, you and I will get up at 5:00 and study your Spanish book until 7:00, six days a week, Sundays off. Get me , brother?"

"But Dad," I utter. "I don't think you understand. It's impossible. I have to get an 85 on the Regents Exam to pass. There's no way. It's too late."

Dad: "I'm not gonna listen to your incessant defeatist attitude, brother. You'd better change your tune, because you are going to pass. Follow me? Is that clear?"

Me, eyes rolling up, and right and then left, sighing, "Okay," softly, disbelievingly.

Dad: "Good. Get a good night's sleep, brother. I'm gonna

wake you up bright and early, man."

And with that, he hoists himself off of the living room sofa where we are seated and goes up the three step stairs into his bedroom. Mom is in bed watching the Merv Griffin show, with a young, new stand up comic as a guest, Richard Pryor. Lying against the walnut bedpost with painted white caned backing, smoking her Lark cigarette, she shushes him as he enters and signals him to wait until the commercial to tell her about the conversation. Pryor is doing his Rumpelstiltskin routine, impersonating young kids acting the part. Mom laughs with her usual soundless open-mouthed squinting grin.

Dad, chuckling machine gun style, then erupting, amused by Pryor's antics, wipes the tears from his eyes as Pryor's routine builds. Then when the Chevy commercial comes on, Dad informs Mom of the Spanish study plan. Mom, too rolls her eyes, sort of like I did earlier.

"Are you sure that's a good idea?" Getting the anticipated affirmative reply, she shrugs her shoulders in weary resignation and lights up another Lark. End of conversation. Turn the channel. It's the Smothers Brothers doing their salute to guns.

The next day my father gets me up at five. We begin our six-week basic training tour for Spanish III, Master Sergeant Milt and his recruit, Private Arnie, feigning motivation, interest and concentration.

Dad, either not knowing or caring, does not attempt to drill me in a language he is not fluent in and doesn't really understand. Grammar, idioms, comprehension, storylines – forget about it! I know it's a joke, but also know protesting is futile. My father is in full-out steamroller mode and I play along, humoring him.

After two weeks, he gives up or stops waking me up. By this time, I am sort of curious to see how I'd do if I did some preparation. So, I study two hours a day for the last four weeks. But in my gut I sense it is probably too late.

On the day of the exam, I feel my only chance is to sit behind an A student. As fate would have it, Roberta Silvestri, an Italian girl with a Puerto Rican mother, an A student, is assigned the seat across from but in front of me. Ronnie and Mac, my two other class compadres taking the tests, look over at me bemused, shaking their heads at my good fortune and their bad luck. They are sitting near kids stupider than they are in Spanish and know they would have to tough it out alone.

Two weeks after the exam, report cards come home. For me, it feels touch and go. I rifle through the mail and find the envelope, all the while Joe the mailman, who knows of my situation, reassures me that I probably passed. Joe is kind of a friend. Sports fan, fight fan. We talk. He's sympathetic. Envelope rips open.

My eyes glance down speedily at the numbers typed on the white sheet. It looks thusly:

	4th quarter grades	Final Exam	Final Grade
Math 11	88	86	82
Chemistry	80	85	80
English 11	84	84	82
Amer. Hist.	90	88	88
Spanish 111	70	86	65
P.E.	90	90	90

"I passed! Whew! Yes!" Both hands fisted pull back toward my stomach and then away. "Yes!!! I am the fucking master. Unbelievable. I can't believe it," out loud to myself as I imitate the famous Russ Hodges announcing Bobby Thompson's famous home run against the Dodgers in '51. The shot heard round the world, scream and shout, "Ahhhhhhhhhhhh," at the top of my lungs. I am one happy man. Relieved. Thank you, Roberta.

You should have seen my father. Ecstatic. I don't have the heart to tell him I cheated, nor the guts, for that matter. Ah! So what? I passed!. That's what counts. Mom makes my favorite dinner that night: brisket, boiled potatoes with tomato gravy and broccoli. Even have a little wine.

After dinner, I get brazen and light a cigarette at the table. Mom and Dad don't blink.

They say it's okay. Better than sneaking around, if I had to smoke. I thank them for their understanding and I am sincere. It's a great night because it feels so good to be in their good graces and to have them proud of me regarding school. I must admit, I really like pleasing them. Although there is no way I can admit that. No way I'm gonna show them I care about what they care about. You kidding? Forget that. But my facial expression must be giving it away. I can't stop grinning and I am aglow with happiness and relief. No summer school. Now, I can get a job in New York City, working in The West Village at my Uncle Bill's Book distribution warehouse. Yes, I thought. Work in the Apple. Mom and Dad think that's a good idea, too.

But first on my mind on this night is having a celebration with my mates. On the phone to Mark and Marla and arrange a date for shy Mark with Marla's friend Becky. The four of us traipse up to Rye Playland to celebrate "School's Out." Marla and Becky are in good moods. They got their usual B's and A's. Mark, his usual A+'s, 98 average on final exams. They are much more blasé and consistent students. For me, tonight is a much bigger deal. Everyone's happy for themselves and for me. Especially Marla. She loves it when I am happy and in a good mood. It usually meant I was nicer to her. Mark didn't care. And Becky, she thinks I'm funny and loves to have fun. She has a mean crush on Mark, too.

They start to make out right away in my back seat with its blue interior seats. With Marla next to me and my arm around her, I'm driving my white Falcon with twenty-seven horsepower up the New

England Thruway to Rye, radio blasting. Young Rascals: "Groovin'," "Happy Together": The Turtles. "The Letter": Box Tops and then, as was my habit, I change the station, without asking, from top 40 AM WABC to FM and the brand new underground station WNEW-FM.

About two minutes from Playland, suddenly it is on. This eerie sounding funereal piano and then that familiar voice of John Lennon singing in a solemn dead serious way. Then midway through the song, you hear McCartney take over the song describing the mundane functions of everyday life, then back to the surrealistic last verse by John. It's nothing we've ever heard the Beatles do before. It's from "Sgt. Peppers," the album that has just come out. And this is the last song on the album. "A Day in the Life."

I stop the car immediately. We listen with religious rapture. Silence. I speak first. "Whew! Unbelievable! Did you hear that? What was that? What a trip!"

Marla: "God, that was great. That was the Beatles?"

Mark: "Pretty far out, pretty poetic. Heavy stuff."

The conversation doesn't go much further than that. Collectively, deep in amazement, Mark takes out an already made joint of leftover Acapulco Gold he had been smoking, lights up with his Zippo lighter, takes a deep, educated toke, a trumpet like sound at the inhale/exhale cusp. Then blows the grey smoke out of his mouth, the three of us marveling at the musical and facial dance display. Clearing his throat, Mark silently with a slight head nod, passes the joint to Becky. Taking it between her thumb and index finger, then squeezing it in her lips, tongue pushing against the paper edge she inhales the cannabis fumes deep into her throat. "Ah, the hit," she mutters, exhaling, extolling the pleasure of the smoke pushing against her throat and down her lungs, Mmmm murmurs and then a slapping sound of her tongue against her teeth echoing off her inner mouth cheeks, clicking.

Marla, next, a look of curiosity and alarm on her face, pauses, betraying her hesitation, tentatively puts the J to her lips then coughs as her inhalation is too strong for her neophyte lungs. Mark and I laugh. Becky puts her hand on Marla's left shoulder clapping against her upper back with her other hand until Marla's coughing ceases.

Marla: "I'm all right. Thanks."

Becky: "It's not funny, Bruch."

Mark: "It's not funny." Then giggling into coughing again.

Waiting. I take the joint from Marla as the silence reasserts its ascendancy in the Falcon. A hundred yards from Rye Playland in the pitch blackness of the summer night, gold stars dotting the sky. I take a poke Bogart style, the joint at the side of my mouth, eyes looking away. Inhaling quickly, smoothly, efficiently. Blowing the smoke out sideways. The noise of the silent night starting to loom louder, engine off, radio off, no wind, bodily movement stilled. Thoughts of the four hermetically sealed organisms now only interrupted by occasional eye gazing. Marla to me, Becky to Mark. Silent, dark void filled almost immediately by a sensation of gut loin circulating in back seat and front seat simultaneously. Instinctively,

Becky moves closer to Mark, sides touching, hands finding each other. Marla, left hand in front seat finds the back of my head as she clutches my curls and then massages my curls with a curly cue motion, pushing herself tight next to me, seated behind the steering wheel. I lean back my head against Marla's hand gently, enjoying the soothing glow and tenderness of her loving touch, drawing her closer to me with my right arm around her, tightly pushing my hand hard against her upper arm, just below her white tee shirt.

My eyes glance compulsively at the rear view mirror as I observe Becky and Mark pretzel-shaped in passionate make out embrace. Enjoying and reacting with increased steam to the scene, I kiss Marla on her ear lobe, slowly nibbling. Pretty soon prone positions dominate. Humping, dry, denim against denim, bra straps coming undone, male hands pushing female hands onto exotic lands. Determined hands moving up the thigh region into the heartland of sweet, liquidy, sweaty environs. Not much resistance tonight, either in the front or back seat. The pot is doing its job. Third base all the way around in minutes. New all-time record here. "Mms" the ricocheting repeated echo of the four of us teenagers as we continue our entwined groping.

Mark, coming up for air, re-invokes the conversation as he bites his lip. "Hey gang," he pitches delightedly, "this is the best. Schools out. I'm with my best pals, a sexy girl, dynamite pot, the Beatles new record. It doesn't get any better than this. Am I wrong or am I right?"

Marla, unable to contain herself, breaks from her clinch with me and hollers, "Yeah, right, Marko," half-jokingly. We all crack up. High pitched sounds abound, hyena-like, as the chortling rapidly escalates in an hysterical chain reaction of hilarity and side splitting inanity.

And we still haven't gotten out of the car yet. Weren't we supposed to go to Playland and celebrate? "What's with us anyway?" I hear myself say. "God, we must be really stoned." We are out of our minds. Wrecked. Really wrecked. "I'm wrecked," I say." "Me, too," everyone else joins in. Marla, giggling, nodding.

Me: "Let's get out of here. I'm starving. Let's get something to eat. Let's get a pizza, right."

"Cool," everyone says in unison. Engine on, lights on. Slowly, we abandon Playland, drive back to Eastchester, pitchers of beer and pizza awaiting. A return to normalcy and familiar environs as we land at Albanese's, our local pizza haunt. Good night. What a night. A splendid time is had by all.

CHAPTER 21

It's Party Time

Marla is drunk when I arrive that night. She's there a while already, drinking Singapore Slings, Becky's parents gone for the weekend. Yes! The Doors are playing on the stereo in the background. "Light My Fire", " Twentieth Century Fox", "The End".

Dancing and prancing. Beer cans, mock tackle football games, boys tackling the girls. Boogeying to be boogeying.

I'm stoked. Mark and Becky are off in some dark bedroom upstairs. Marla hugs me deliriously as we walk in the black painted front door leading directly into their beige decorated living room. "Bruch, I love you." Marla clings tight to me with both arms around my neck. "Bruch...Bruch...Fuck me."

"What?" I say pushing her off me. "You're drunk. How much booze have you had?"

Marla: "Who cares, Bruch? Please Bruch, I'm tired of being a virgin. Bruch. Do it, Arnie. Come on."

Stunned, I can't think. I don't know what to say. This is supposed to be the moment I've been waiting for. Now it's here but this is not how I want to feel. This doesn't feel good. Doesn't seem right. I'm thinking, she's drunk. It's gross. This isn't a turn on. It's gross. I hate this. I can't stand this. This sucks.

Me: "Marla, you're shitfaced. I'm not gonna fuck you. This is ridiculous. It's not fair. It wouldn't be fair. I don't want to feel like I'm taking advantage of you just because you're drunk. I want you to want to do it with me 'cause you're ready to do it not cause you're drunk. Forget it. I'm not gonna do it. Let's go to the bathroom. You look awful."

Marla: "Bruch, I'm sorry. Don't hate me."

Me: "I don't hate you, but..."

Marla: "I'm sick. I got to go to the bathroom. Hurry."

Racing to the bathroom, we get there just as she wretches into the porcelain bowl. All better. I hold her as we recline on the floor next to the toilet bowl. Marla, softly weeping. Feeling better, gradually. We take a walk outside of Becky's house and then I drive her home. I drop her off, kiss her on the cheek and she gives me a big hug. I tell her to get some sleep, patting her on top of the head. She softly purrs.

"I will, thanks, Arnie. I love you, Bruch."

Me: "Feel better, Marla." I backpedal away from the door, slowly waving good night. Getting back into my Falcon, I sigh, feeling two parts good about myself and one part wretched. I'm cursed, I think, I'm never gonna get laid. Ah, booze is a drag. I think I'm gonna stick to pot and cigarettes. Booze is so fucking sloppy. It's gross, what it does to you. I drive home and go to sleep.

Two weeks later on a Saturday afternoon in mid-July, Marla is over at my house watching the baseball game with me. Pete Rose's Reds vs. Leo Durocher's Cubs. Rich Izo, a rookie pitcher for the Cubs is on the mound. He's my older brother Dave's best friend's brother. So, his being on the mound gives the game added punch. Marla and I are in a mellow mood and not drinking, just lying on my parents bedspread folded up in each other. Just hanging out on a lazy summer day. Relaxing. My parents are away for the weekend, visiting my younger brother in the Berkshires at sleepaway camp. The house is mine, all to myself. Zee, our housekeeper, has just left to go home for the weekend.

CHAPTER 22

I Think We're Alone Now

Game of the week. Curt Gowdy, Sandy Koufax and Joe Garagiola are discussing the new rookie Cub sensation, Rich Izo, "our friend." Rich's gonna have dinner with us the following weekend when the Cubs come into town to play the Mets for a four game series. But this game they're winning 5-2 in the bottom of the seventh. Marla and I are doing our usual make out routine. First base, second base and then the battle over whether to advance to third on a "passed ball" or a "balk." Ron Santo, the Cubs' third baseman and cleanup hitter flies out. Marla pushes my hand away from her pubes. Ernie Banks doubles down the line. I grab her hand and place it in my underpants, holding it there firmly then moving her hand in a rotating friction fashion. She's not thrilled with the idea, but not exactly pulling her hand away either. I sneak my hand back toward her pubic bone, a little off the mark, skimming against curly cue hairs and orifice damp. Marla pushes me away once, twice and then stops and lets me leave it there. We're in position now.

Like Jackie Robinson, leading off third, ten steps off base, Bob Turley goes into full windup. It's a tense moment. What's Jackie gonna do? Will he run? Will he bluff? There's no telling really. He's poised. Eyes on Turley. Purposeful, directed. Ready. Turley winds up as his glove reaches his chin, his eyes a flurry of dust and a thick black torrent racing down the third baseline. Hurried, he fires high to Yogi Berra, slightly off the plate, first base side. Jackie slides, spikes high. Yogi tags him.....Safe. Primed. Randy Hundley doubles, Rich Izo in his own cause rifles one up the middle for a single. I take off my underpants. Don Kissinger walks. Off go Marla's panties. She assists me, as Glenn Beckert also walks loading up the bases. Bringing up Billy Williams, the sweet swinger. Bases loaded, Williams up. 6-2 the score. Bottom of the eighth. All quiet. Naked. The tension is mounting. Ball one. Wrigley is standing. Come on, Billy, blaring from the T.V. Two balls, one strike. Williams' bat is still. Bourbon fires. Thwack. Sound of bat on ball, sweet spot into Billy's wheelhouse, drives it deep to right, way back, deep, "that ball is outta here, grand slam." Mmm. Contact. The Eagle has landed.

CHAPTER 23

Back to School Senior Year

Two days after Labor Day, the first day of the school year, September '67, I drive Marla home en route to a schoolyard softball game between the north end Jews and the south end Italians for $20 a man. I'm playing center field and leading off. Mac is in left, batting third. Ricky at first, batting second. Mark at second bats sixth. The Italians are big, bigger in size and muscularity than we are. Lots of gymnasts and wrestlers. We're soccer and baseball. They have just won the Eighteen and Under Rec. League softball championships. We didn't enter. That summer most of us had been working, partying, getting stoned or going to the track. None of our crew had been playing ball.

Both sides smoke cigarettes. My team, eight out of ten smoke Marlboros. Theirs, nine out of ten. The game is scheduled to start at 2:30, but first I drop Marla off at her house at noon. We're on double session. That means the seniors get out of class by noon. We start at 7:30. Five majors and gym. Six periods. No frills and you're out of there. Bare bones high school.

Marla can't make it to the game but she wishes she could. She knows the greasers are bringing their girlfriends and their souped-up cars. We have no female presence on the Jewish side. Just as well, I say, it would be too distracting. As I drop Marla off, she invites me in. It's been four weeks since the Cubs game thing and a week since we've seen each other.

The vibes are tense. Whenever I don't see Marla or speak to her on the phone regularly, she gets insecure, like I don't care about her or I've found someone else.

Actually, I am dating someone else, a sophomore Irish girl named Jean O'Bannion. I met her at a Beach Club dance and she's pretty fast for her age. Fifteen, drinks like a fish and smokes cigarettes. And her parents let her, too. Pretty sophisticated. Reads Camus. In fact, she turned me on to *The Stranger*. I've just spent the last weekend home alone with the book and it's probably the most significant book I've ever read. Existential angst. Aloneness. Right up my alley. Jean O'Bannion, she's hip. Dresses sort of beat, sort of hippie. She wears miniskirts, tight tee shirts, sandals, fishnet stockings. She has the hint of the bad girl down, just enough. Somehow, Marla has gotten word of it and she's pissed. I mean we're supposed to be going steady practically one year now. She's only gone out with two guys since we started going together. Both guys, my friends, Jeff and Mac. Thanks guys. If they fucked her, I'd kill myself. They didn't. I thought the cherry was intact during the Cubs game. To be fair, I've also dated a couple of her friends, Lena and Becky. But, they're loyal to Marla, hence no action. More than I can say for Jeff. I don't think Mac did much. He claims they just made out. He says Marla led him into it to get even with me for one of my no phoning, no seeing, no communication routines that hurt her feelings. I'll get you back, sorties.

Anyway, this stuff is pretty routine for my crowd, in the mid '60's, at the cusp of major changes pending in the culture. It's the tail end of the old, transitioning into the new socially, sexually, attitudinally. So, I figure we're even. Marla belatedly agrees. We both begrudgingly cop to our past indiscretion without going into details and kiss and make up. All is forgiven. This clears the air and puts us both in a good mood again.

Marla even makes me lunch. Turkey sandwich on rye with a root beer chaser. Yeah, I love it when we're getting along. I just wish she would be a little more intellectual. That's about the only complaint about her that I can come up with but intellectual matters are starting to become important to me. I'm starting to become excited about learning again. I mean in school. Not just on my own. But Marla's too, I don't know, – basic. Case Mase: sweet, sexy, fun, loving, nice, a good dancer, too. Into Black people. Black soul music. Good arm. Good baseball player. But she's not really into reading. I mean she doesn't have a clue about *The Stranger* or, for that matter, *The Brothers Karamazov*, another book I've just read that summer while working for my Uncle Bill in The West

Village. But that's just not her. It bugs me. I need to be around girls who think.

Jean O'Bannion definitely does. Ooo, she is sexy, too. I mean, I don't know, it's like I think, I'm, you know, outgrowing Marla. I don't know. Who knows? I don't want to think about this. I'm lost in a trance.

"Bruch," Marla interrupts my reverie, "wake up. You're always spacing out. What are you thinking about?"

"I don't know," I lie.

Marla: "Bruch. Do you love me? I love you."

Me: "Why do you have to ask me this all the time? I hate this."

Marla: "Because, I need to know. I'm scared. You never say!"

Me: "Come on. I don't want to talk about this again. You know I think you're the best."

Marla: "So why don't you tell me you love me then?"

Me, sighing: "Can we drop it?"

Marla, hurt and dejected: "Okay. I wish you'd treat me better, Bruch. I miss you. I love you so much. Kiss me."

I comply.

Marla: "Kiss me the right way, you schmuck."

Reluctantly, I open my mouth.

Marla: "Bruch, hold me tighter, tighter, tighter, hmmm. That's better. I love hugging you Bruch."

Me: "Me, too."

Marla: "I love you."

I hug her harder.

Marla: "I love you so much."

The hugging continues.

Me: "Mm, feels good."

Marla kisses me hard on the mouth. We collapse on the kitchen floor.

Marla: "Let's go upstairs, Arnie. To my room."

Me: "All right."

We dart upstairs, re-collapsing together on her bed. Volcanic embers, kindling red, orange rays, writhing, shirts off. Hungry... greedy.

Marla: "Mmm."

Me: "Mmm."

Marla: "Oh, God."

Me: "Mmm."

Now we're stark-naked. No doubt this time about what's gonna happen. Last month's escapade at my house during the Cubs game cinched the matter. We're going in, fellas. All systems go. There is a relaxed quality to the passion this time, unlike any of our prior encounters. Not just passion. But some actual enjoyment. An almost leisurely quality. Languorous, watery, cool, refreshing alternating with hot sweaty, funky musty exchanges. Synchronized swimming with bodies touching.

"I'm gonna use a condom." I say out loud. "OK," I say, half asking, half telling.

"Not yet, I'm scared... Arnie. Please."

" Okay," I say.

"I want to do it, but I'm scared."

"Yeah," I say as I think to myself, here I am again. On the launch pad with the countdown aborted at T minus one. The Trojan will have to live and fight another day. Slightly annoyed. But what else is new. I'm sick of this shit, I think. But I feign understanding.

We light up our Marlboros anyway. We inhale expertly. Bogart and Bacall, as if. I put my dungarees back on, give Marla a soft kiss on the lips. She wishes me good luck with the greasers and I leave for the game.

CHAPTER 24

Ethnic Baseball Game

We arrive a half hour before game time. The greasers arrive just before game time in a cloud of smoke and turbo red. And in uniform. Black tee shirts, packs of Marlboros rolled up in their shirt sleeves over their biceps, black dungarees, black high tops, a la the Boston Celtics, while we are in blue denims, dungarees. That's as uniform as we get. Half the greasers, wear baseball hats, mostly Yankee, some Mets. Both sides smoking their asses off. Coughing rules. The Yids win the odds or evens choose and elect to play on our home turf, Albert Leonard Jr. High.

They lead off. Jack Fresco pops to short. Their next two batters fly to Mac in left and to me in center. Routine fly balls. In my head, I'm announcing the game, as usual. "Leading off and batting first for the North End Yid Meisters, #24 Arnold 'Ace' Pacer Bruchner." Deep drive off the left field fence on the second pitch. Home run. Mark follows and hits an inside the park home run straight up the middle, low liner. Mac follows, batting third with a tape measure shot to right. "No doubt about it." Over the fence. Jeff, Rob and Stu continue the onslaught with a homer, ground rule double, and double down the left field line. After the inning is over. Jews 8. Greasers 0.

We are never headed. They concede after five innings and pay us our $20. They're gentlemen and depart silently with a modicum of pride and self-respect intact. We don't gloat or trash them. Our bats have done the talking and they know it. Nothing to say. Even their girlfriends have stopped clicking their gum before leaving in their souped-up Chevys and what have you. I guess we're pretty good ballplayers, if not tough hombres.

They don't challenge us again. Actually, the greasers get friendlier with us and even start partying with us at pot parties, which are starting to proliferate around this time. A big social opening and unifier between the Blacks, Italians and Jews. It's fun, nice. Dopers of the world unite. You have nothing to lose but your ethnic identities, racial hostilities, turf and class loyalties, and motivation to do anything. This is the start of the best four months of my life. Past or present. Autumn '67. You had to be there. I was. I'll tell you about it.

CHAPTER 25

Levy and Satcher

Mac, Mark and I, mark our slaughter of the Italians that weekend by heading down to the Café Au Go to check out Eric Andersen and the Young Bloods. "Thirsty Boots," "Violets of Dawn," "Grizzly Bear," and "Get Together." These songs memorialize that evening for us. Crispy yearnings, idealistic hope, peace and love. Romance. Stop the bombing. Gimme some pussy. Sweet musky patchouli-like aromas permeate the air. We head back home, stoned out and blissful, in sweet musings. Glide off the train in Scarsdale and into Mac's 404 1962 Peugeot and book back to Mac's house just in time for "The Harder they Fall," famous for being Bogart's last movie. I must say the three of us ate that movie up.

Monday next. Levy's first period class. "Problems of American Democracy." Liz Delmonico sits behind me as Levy puts us in a circle and sits with us, breaking up traditional teacher/student boundaries and hierarchies, symbolically indicating the collapse of authority relations between student and teacher. This might be the first time in the history of New Rochelle High that a teacher sits with his students in a circle. We hear he gets shit for it from the administrators. But he doesn't care. He's too old and financially secure to care. Levy's a retired "schmatah" business owner, who came into teaching in his mid-sixties. I hear that an old lefty from the history department at NRHS went to bat for him and the heat died down.

Levy conducts his class like a graduate seminar except there are twenty-eight students. No papers. No tests. Just group discussion and oral presentations. No written homework, just reading articles. Levy probably doesn't want to spend his time reading student papers and figures senior year should be fun. So do we. The guy is stimulating and his approach with the class is Socratic. Lots of challenging of assumptions. The class loves him and his style because we have thoughtful, philosophical discussions. He makes us think. He recommends articles and books to augment our discussions, but they're recommendations, not required for our grade. It's only suggested. Levy digs me. I get an A+.

My psychology teacher is cool, too. These are the first really good teachers I've had in a long time. Man, what a drought. Now, the drought is over. I have two ace teachers in one semester. My LUCK is changing. I know. I can feel it. It's real. I get straight A's that semester and more importantly, I really am beginning to enjoy formal academic learning, maybe for the first time – ever. I actually look forward to the assignments, and I don't even cut one class. A major change for me particularly after my horrendous tenth and eleventh grade academic performance. A major shift in attitude and behavior. I am much more respectful, fun loving, good-natured, yet serious-minded and focused both in and out of the classroom. Teachers like me. Parents, too. They compliment me on my burgeoning maturity – intellectually and emotionally.

Socially, things are shifting positively as well. Women of very different stripes and types are showing interest and flirting. Intellectuals, Italian beauties, hippy-beat artsy women are talking to me like Liz for instance, who sits right behind me in Levy's class, first period. She's gorgeous. Dirty blonde hair, wavy, long. Fishnet stockings, short miniskirts, bright, yet unpretentious and unassuming. Grounded. Smiles at me. I am a star in this class. I swear I am. A star. First time ever, for me – P.E. excepted.

There's this chemistry between Levy and me, like father and son. He's 65, I'm 17. Whatever. The guy brings out the best in me. He convenes serious thoughtful, passionate debates on capital punishment, the separation of church and state, the system of checks and balances. He knows how to get at the ethical and moral components behind the legal facets. We spend a long time on the Kitty Genovese case, which is in all the papers. The case seems to crystalize a lot of controversies that bring out political, ideological, moral and psychological differences among people. We discuss what each of us as passersby would do if we heard screaming sounds on the streets of New York. Levy forces us to be honest and confront our own selfish impulses to avoid trouble. He helps us contrast our idealistic sense of how we would act, our heroic certainties about ourselves versus how we might actually respond when seeing a victim being hurt. The issues we discuss spill over into discussions between me and my friends. It relates directly to our own concerns.

My psychology class is a trip, too. This girl Greta is in it. Sort of a "dog" on the surface, but super-bright, feisty, funny hippyish and radical. Anti-war. Goes out with Blacks, smokes dope. Gets straight A's. A shoo-in for Vassar. Puts out an angry vibe and known to be loose, sexually and not known to be embarrassed or ashamed about it either. Hates jocks and greasers and not real thrilled with preppies or nerds either. She likes hippies, artists, intellectuals, non-conformists. She likes me. I like her. She tells me that I don't fit into any of the usual molds. Not really straight. Not really a jock, not really a preppy, not nerdy, but a little of all of those things and kind of none of those things. I say the same about her but not as eloquently. We connect.

Satcher, the psychology teacher, is the Ernest Hemingway of the school. He looks like Teddy Roosevelt with his handlebar moustache and rides a Harley-Davidson and seems to be a rugged individualist but he's also getting his doctorate in Latin American History at Columbia. His teaching style is no nonsense. He's teaching us about "behavior". With my nine months of shrinking, I'm into it and drink it up like a camel at an oasis. The whole course load is an academic oasis. I never knew learning could be like this. Exciting, alive. My enthusiasm knows no bounds. I'm reading. Reading the front pages of The Times, not just the sports and entertainment page, and understanding it. I'm starting to have informed opinions.

My friends, too, are tuning into the political and social scene going on. Vietnam, Black Power, the new Civil Rights strand, civil liberties, campus unrest, all that stuff.

That October, Mac, Mark, Greta and I head down to D.C. on a bus to attend our first anti-war demonstration, henceforth known as the "March on the Pentagon" that Norman Mailer later writes about and publishes a year later in *Armies of the Night.* It is exciting and scary both and gets violent near the Pentagon. The four of us go with Mac's parents, some old time lefties from the thirties and forties. We stay away from the violence, although I must admit that that part of the demonstration is by far the most compelling and scary to me. The unrest, the speeches, crowds, the mingling, the sense of instant community is cool, too.

Mark, although into it, is by far the most skeptical about the whole thing. He's anti-establishment all right but he's pretty suspicious of the arrogant self-righteous pronouncements he's hearing from people at the demonstration. He's put off by the anti-war demonstrators' sureness of conviction. The rest of us are much more susceptible to the passion and the opportunity to vent an anger that seems to be bursting from inside of us. The war in Vietnam is providing us with a good target to vent our spleens. Not that the anger isn't legitimate, mind you. It's just that Mark would first off question the depth of some of their commitment, second, the "rightness" of their positions and third, and last, this peace and love "junk." Mark doesn't see the spouters of peace and love behaving much differently than the older generation or the pro war hawks. Mark is like a thorn in our sides. He's a pinprick to our tendency to get carried away in our enthusiasm that the revolution or something is coming . He's a drag. But he forces us to think. But who wants to think? It's much more fun being a partisan spouting rhetoric. Let Mark stay detached and outside but it seems much less alive.

After the Pentagon demonstration, I become even more involved and informed. I start reading The Times front page every day, buy and read books on Vietnam by Bernard Fall and David Schoenbrun and become more vocal in and out of class.

My parents, by this time, I must say, are sympathetic and supportive of this change in me. They too have become anti-war doves, anti-Johnson and sympathetic to the anti-war movement on and off the college campuses. Of course, there is still plenty to argue with them about, mostly at the kitchen table. Like the issue of violence versus non-violence and the question about the nature of capitalism, regularly occurring topics for dinner discourse. My teachers are impressed with my increasing knowledge of the situation in Vietnam and its historical context, Satcher, the psych teacher, in particular. He selects Greta and me to go with him to his Pace College graduate history seminar, which he is co-leading to discuss the "Generation Gap." He picks us, he tells us, because he views us as two of the most articulate spokespersons for the emerging youth culture that's been burgeoning since the "British Invasion" and "Free Speech Movement" in '64. Satcher sees clearly the generational divide between us seventeen-year-olds and his grad students, who are in their early to mid-twenties. Satcher, himself is 37, of another generation: "The Silent Generation" as they came to be known. They grew up post World War II, Korea, Eisenhower, Man in the Grey Flannel Suit and Beats era. He's clearly fascinated by the divide he observes between those born just before 1946 and those after.

Satcher lines us up in front of the class where ten grad students, with short hair and pleated skirted students sit. Scraggly, dungaree-wearing, scruffy high school students sit facing them. Satcher in tie, shirt sleeves, cuffed chinos, Weejuns brown shoes, moderates the discussion.

Male grad student to Greta: "Can you define the Generation Gap happening today?"

Greta: "Yeah, it's easy. It's a revolution of values, lifestyle and politics."

Male grad student: "Why now?"

Me: "Because the war is going on, people are being killed on both sides and the war is wrong. Because of the Civil Rights movement, but mostly because parents are out of touch with their kids.

Female Grad student: "What do you mean out of touch?"

Greta: "What we mean is parents today don't understand what is happening to us. They can't relate to the pressures we face. They're interested in making money and having comfort. Their values are out of touch with what is important to us."

Female grad student: "What is important to your generation?"

Greta: "I think it's different for different people, which I think is part of what is important. The right to be different."

Same grad student: "You mean non-conformist?"

Me: "Sort of, but more than that. Something is drastically wrong with this country, both in terms of our politics and how we treat each other. We are merely saying as much with our music, clothes, protests and drug experimenting.

Another male grad student: "How are drugs part of your revolution?"

Greta: "They tell us about possibilities. What potentialities for happiness exist."

Same male grad student: "Isn't that a cop out from facing the responsibilities of the world and the reality of your lives?

Greta: "Maybe, maybe not."

Grad student: "I don't understand."

Me: "Well, it's like this. It all depends on how drugs are used, by whom and for what purpose. It can be a cop out or it can be a door into the future. It all depends."

Grad student: "I am confused and perplexed. You seem to be criticizing the older generation and the so-called 50's, Silent Generation for their passivity and conformity. Isn't smoking pot and taking LSD doing the same thing but in a different way?"

Greta: "Maybe, but I don't think so. Like Aldous Huxley said in the *Doors of Perception*, some people will use drugs to tune out and escape and others will use drugs as a tool for self-knowledge and higher consciousness."

Grad student: "Yeah, but what about social change? You can't change the world stoned on pot."

Me: "That's true. But politics as usual, communist or capitalist ain't gonna cut it anymore. The personal is political. The political is personal. How we treat each other is a political act. You dig?"

Grad student: "Not exactly. I don't think I dig. Actually, I think you kids are full of it. Really, affluent, spoiled middle class posturers that have been lucky enough to enjoy the fruits of your parents' labor and now you are biting the hand that feeds you, your folks. That's what I think. You DIG?"

Greta: "Whew. That's pretty heavy. And what are you? A future man in the Grey Flannel suit, don't make waves, corporate, company automaton kind of guy. Gee, I wish I could be like you. You know what, Dylan had you guys pegged. You're half dead, dazed zombies. Just give me my house in the suburbs, Barbie-doll wife and scotch and soda when I come home. Yippee. Let me be like you."

Satcher, sensing the rising tension and hostility, interrupts and tries to restore order. "Come on now. This is getting a little heated and personal. Let's see if we can kind of stay on the issues without getting into personal attacks. This topic is apparently very loaded. But let's see if we can stay focused on the subjects at hand. I, myself would like to know from Greta and Arnie where they think this generation stands on the issue of non-violence."

But now the energy and intensity in the room shifted. Greta and I pull back emotionally from the subject. The grad students, taking the cue from Satcher ask their questions in a much more careful and reserved manner. But as a consequence, the discussion soon becomes more lifeless. The questions are more respectful and less pointed. The answers from us more vague as we disengage. Too bad, I think. I wish Satcher would have done more with getting the two groups to look at where all the emotional heat had been coming from, but my sense is that we are challenging each other's pretenses, revered beliefs, and that neither side like it much or can handle it very well. Such are the times. People's nerves are on edge. Lots of sensitivity, defensiveness and attacking can be seen from all parties in this cultural and generational divide. People's values and lifestyles are on the line. Rarely are people respectful for long. We talk for another forty five minutes or so with the grad students about hair, rock 'n' roll, Vietnam, the draft, capitalism and drugs, again. The gulf truly exists. A difference in age of only five, six or seven years is a chasm when it comes to our differing world views and the hostility and enmity are palpable. We are confident, arrogant, full of ourselves, cocksure in our beliefs, angry and accusing in our attacks. They, the last vestiges of the Silent Generation, skeptical, analytical, maybe a little scared of what we represent, maybe a little envious. Whatever it is, there is little affection.

At the end, Satcher congratulates us on our articulateness, gutsiness and our willingness to stand by our beliefs and respond to what at times was difficult questioning. He doesn't get on our case for going after the grad students. Satcher sees us as defending ourselves and our turf, so to speak, and retaliating in kind. Greta and I are quite high coming back from Pleasantville that day. Soon, Greta and I will be dating. A week later, it is Christmas break.

CHAPTER 26

Christmas Break
The Rochellean Stag

Marla looks beautiful. Foxily attired, in woolen miniskirt with matching stockings. Me, in my dark three-piece green suit. Three degree weather, snowflakes, steam breath, fresh night. Off in the Falcon. I'm in a good mood. Marla's in a good mood. Pick up Mac and Sue and they're in a good mood. Why not? School's out. Senior year and life is great. Riding over to the Fountainhead Restaurant in the Wykagyl section of northern New Rochelle where the dance is to be held. Marla is in the shotgun seat, Mac and Sue in the back. Marlboros going, singing to the AM radio. "WMCA." "Magical Mystery Tour. "Roll up." "Cheer up, sleepy dream, oh what can it mean to a daydream believer" – "Incense and Peppermint" – "Sittin' on the Dock of the Bay, watching the tide rollaway hmmm." "Roll up. Roll up". Yocks. Laughin'. Nonsensical patter. We get there. Hundreds of couples dressed to the nines. The local band inside is belting out the Rascals' "Love is a Beautiful Thing." Couples are frugging, doing the boogaloo and funky Broadway. The Blacks, Italians, Irish and the Jews, Straights and Heads. The slide rule crowd and the greasers, jocks, artsy fartsies and politicos. We're all there. It's glorious. Dancin'. Rock 'n' roll. Bumpin' and grindin'. Yes, we are! Yes, we are! Smokin' a J, a little 7 and 7, too. Whoops... It's midnight.

Time to head to the college diner for post-game (dance) breakfast. Mac and me. Marla and Sue. Just about the best pals you can have, I swear. Next thing you know, it's 3:00 am. Havin' a ball. Drop Sue off. Drop Mac off next. Now it's Marla and me in her driveway, sitting in my car with the lights out, motor off, snowflakes falling heavier now. Front seat, radio on, in a clench. Someone opens Marla's car door.

"Come out of this car this instant young lady! The nerve of you coming home this late. Now, get in the house this minute. As for you, young man. It'll be when hell freezes over till you see my daughter again. YOUNG MAN. GOOD NIGHT!"

I'm like, stunned then incredulous. What happened? It's a blur. One minute Marla and I are snug and cozy in the car, the next like," Whoa." I turn my motor on, back out of the driveway quick. Peel rubber, as derisively as it can be done, which with a Ford Falcon is not that easy, and head home, a full two blocks away. Adios – Marla.

Next day, I wake up. I can't decide whether to feel bad about the Marla situation or liberated. I don't think about it too long. The next thing I know I'm on the phone to Greta from Satcher's class and make a date with her for that night. Then I call Jean O'Bannion, the sophomore Irish beauty who I have seen over the previous summer, and make a date for the next night, Sunday, Christmas Eve.

Ah, Greta. I pick her up at her house that night. She's psyched and suggests we go to see a movie, "The Graduate." She's dressed in black turtleneck, black boots and black scarf. Cool. We head to the RKO Theatre downtown. The movie blows us both out. It's right on the generational pulse of what we're all thinking, feeling and experiencing right now. The Simon and Garfunkel music is great and makes us both really long to go to California, particularly Berkeley where a lot of the movie takes place. The movie says it all about the Generation Gap.

We immediately head for Albo's for pizza after, where they serve you beer even if you're underage and we do take advantage of that. Hold hands in the booth. Vibes are good. We head back to my house and the den where I usually watch T.V. The parents are in bed. We make out on the couch. Take off Greta's bra, no resistance. Relaxed, natural. She wants to take her time, she says but at the same time makes it clear that she is not reluctant to go further at some future date. She says she wants to let "it" build. I say, "cool," more meaning it than not, and I drive her home and we say goodnight. I'm gleeful about future dates with Greta and the great good time I've had with someone who I feel is on the same wavelength as me.

Back to my house. I'm reeling. Tomorrow, I'm going on a date with Jean O'Bannion. Three women, you hear, I've got three now. I just finished the semester with an A average. My parents think I'm hot stuff. People want to know me. I'm a happenin' dude. Yee Hah.

Christmas Eve day comes around quickly and I'm up by noon. Because of the holiday no games today. The parents are home reading the Times as usual. My older brother Dave is home from Madison, Wisconsin, senior year, just off the heels of a major campus protest. Dow Chemical is on campus, military recruitment hassles, sit-ins, the takeover of the administration building, etc. Dave's a radical intellectual type. Whatever. We're hangin' tonight but later I'm going over to Jean O'Bannion's, my little sixteen-year-old Irish blonde honey.

She's cute, beat, poetic. Whatever. I am attracted to her. and she is to me. Come on now. This is gonna be fun in part because I know Jean's parents are a trip. That night, X-Mas Eve, no one in church, Jean is feeling a bit religious, asks me if I want to go to church with her. I say, "Yeah," having never been inside of a Catholic Church before. So, into the Falcon, off to the town next door, Larchmont, and we stop at the church where a folk mass is happening. Guitars. Short service. Cool. Heading back to her house, following the mass, we're making out at every red light. We're a little tipsy on Xmas wine. Jean in her tipsy state can't stop saying "puffy." She sticks out her cheeks, blows them out and then says, "PUFFY." It strikes her as funny. Me, too. I guess because I'm tipsy too.

Back at her house, we smoke cigarettes, listen to jazz, drink wine and make out. Pretty degenerate stuff. I kind of like it. This family is not your typical north end Jewish professional business-like middle class family stuff. No way. South end – Boho, literary, Wild Irish Rose, edgy, struggling, worrying about money. All that stuff. A very different scene here than what I am used to. Their house is dirtier, more cluttered. I like it a lot. It seems really homey somehow. I am tired of that stable boring, Jewish, comfortable lifestyle of my family, my friends and neighbors. This is different. It seems better, more open, loose, free. Then "Home James," pretending I'm my own chauffeur. I find the road, bleary-eyed at 3:00 in the morning. Back to the staid north end where all is quiet. Asleep, actually. And I soon go there as well.

Three nights later, I receive a call from Marla informing me that the ban on me is lifted. Party time. We can go out again. I inform her of a party that night at a guy's house named Oren, a freshman home from college. There will be lots of people and she is up for it. I ring her doorbell at 8:00 p.m. and her father answers it, looking sheepish.

"Come on in, young man." I do. He commences, " I owe you an apology for my behavior with you last week. It was out of line."

"Accepted," I say. "No big deal," and we shake hands. Awkward silence. "Where's Marla?" I ask at the very moment that she appears from behind the bannister heading down the carpeted stairs.

"Ready," she shouts.

"All right," I reply.

Off we go to the Christmas party. A larger mixture than usual of age groupings are there that night. Sixteen to twenty-two is the age spread. Marla looks cute, especially so that night. And me: I'm doin' my usual blasé routine, feigning interest towards the artsy, intellectual crowd, hanging with my mates, Mac, Mark and my tennis rival/buddy, Rick.

Rick's making a rare party appearance. Rick hangs with the Ivy League, intellectual, artsy scene. Tennis, reading good books, the whole trip. He's class treasurer, on a collision course with Harvard. His brother is already a senior there, greasing the wheel for him. My brother Dave, ain't doin' nothin' for me. In fact, he just walked in with his girlfriend Kiki Dupont, tipsy. He's glad handing. Schmoozing. High five's me. Grabs Marla and they do the frug together to James Brown. "I Feel Good." Mr. Dynamite. James Brown.

Gimme a break, Dave. He dances like Howdy Doody, playing the violin in slow motion. No hop at all. Marla dances well and displays lots of enthusiasm and good cheer. Me: I'm on the sidelines "Drinkin' wine, spodiodi, drinkin' wine." The party is crowded and filled with smoke. It's noisy with lots of movement. Time passes. Where's Marla? My groggy head sails after what seems like a long idle in Never Land. Fear encases me. I move around the house, opening doors carelessly. Then, I open one and there's Marla on a bed with brother Dave. I'm blown out, can't speak.

"Bruch," Marla cries out, as I walk out the bedroom door. Grabbing me by the shoulders from behind. "Don't go, please." She's wailing now. I'm moving, not saying anything. Still groggy, sort of. "I, we, he, I don't know, got drunk and we were..."

Me: "Spare me, will you?"

Marla: "Bruch, I'm sorry."

Me: "It's okay."

Just then, Dave appears from behind us and puts an arm around both of us.

Dave: "My man. I'm sorry."

Me: "That's okay."

Dave, looking sheepish, and is in an alcoholic fog as well. Me: "You know what, man? You shouldn't drink. You do fucked up things when you do."

Dave: "My man, you're right. You're right."

Me: "I know I'm right. So where's Kiki? I think I'll go hit on her. Where is she?"

Dave: "I don't know."

Marla overhears and says, "Come on, Bruch."

Me: "What?"

Marla : "Bruch. Come on."

Me: "Don't talk to me, either one of you."

I leave, looking for Dave's date, Kiki. She's occupied dancing with my friend Mac. I watch them doing the Funky Broadway, then head back to the kitchen. Marla corrals me, puts her arms around me and says, lips an inch apart, "Bruch, please forgive me. I shouldn't drink."

Me: "Yeah."

And we kiss. Marla tries to assuage her guilt and I say, "I'm disgusted. Let's leave."

Marla nods submissively. We put our coats on and are gone in a flash, back to Marla's house. There, we sit in her living room talking about our relationship. It feels lousy. She's apologetic. Me, I'm turned off but kind of reveling and milking my leverage. Then the discussion turns frank. I realize I am talking about how the relationship is not meeting my needs, neither sex-wise nor communication-wise. Marla looks heartbroken. But it's true. I can't help how I feel. The booze nudges the words along. Next thing I know I break up with her. She's crying, sobbing. I hug her painfully and then drive the two blocks back home where brother Dave and Kiki are in our living room drinking Grand Marnier.

It's 2:00 a.m. I join them, listening to their conversation, silently, downing Grand Marniers. Mom and Dad are asleep in the deep upstairs. Dave and Kiki are talking about college, Vietnam, I don't know what. New Rochelle, how it hasn't changed, how it has... I'm bummed. Sad, heavy feeling, like numbing the pain. I don't tell them Marla and I have broken up. I say good night. Go up to my room, with the spins.

The next day, I see Jean O'Bannion, my wild Irish rose, then Greta the day after that. It's still good, but slightly less fun now. New Year's Eve, I'm with Greta and we're sitting out in my car getting ready to go to another freshman college party given by a kid Greta knows, when out of nowhere, Marla appears, seemingly out of the shadows, yelling and running. She puts her arms around me and says, "Happy New Year's, Bruch." And then is gone with her date. Weird. It bums me out even more than I was before. We head into Greta's friend's house and I'm stunned, thrown back into myself. I size up the crowd and given my mood, feel out of place and critical of this preppy, Ivy League scene. I'm doing my James Dean/Jack Kerouac routine. Sullen, superior and hostile. People are keeping their distance. That's fine with me. I want to be alone anyway. I drive Greta home at around 12:30. I'm bummed and alienated from Greta as well. I give her a peck on the cheek and say good night. Happy New Year.

CHAPTER 27

O.S.U. Here I Come

Three days later, the envelope arrives. A thick one, addressed from Columbus. Standing between the front door and foyer, I rip open the letter with my mother walking out of the kitchen to see, catching the glee in my eye just before she hears the yelp, "YES!" I happily rush to hug her. "I'm in Mom. I'm in."

"Oh, Arnie, I'm so glad, sweetie pie. It's such a relief. You should be proud of yourself. Mazel Tov."

"Thanks, Ma," I offer back gratefully. Wooh, does that feel good.

"Now your father and I can go to Arizona in peace. Congratulations."

"I didn't know you were that worried about me getting in," I say, sort of surprised.

"Well, I didn't want to say anything 'cuz I thought it might put more pressure on you than you already felt. Getting into college is a big thing. And your dad and I know how hard you have worked this past year to get your grades up. I think seeing Dr. Chidas has been really good for you. What do you think?"

"Yeah, I think so, too. Yeah, definitely. I feel better and I feel more confident. Yeah, definitely, been a good thing."

"Well, I'm just so proud and relieved, Arnie. Now I'm really looking forward to that vacation with your father. It's like a weight has been lifted."

"Me, too, big time," I say. "I'm sure Dad will be relieved as well, don't you think, Ma?"

"Of course," Mom says, "it'll be a weight off his mind, too.

I'm gonna go finish packing. We have to leave at noon tomorrow and I want to be prepared. You know how your father is about being ready when we go on trips." It was one of my father's trademarks. Arriving at the airport two hours in advance is his claim to fame and causes a tremendous amount of anxiety and tension for the entire family before our trips. I am glad to not be going with them for a variety of reasons, that merely being one of them. After all, it was their twenty-fifth anniversary celebration. It was for them. Plus, I didn't want to leave my friends and my life in New Rochelle particularly now that it was getting good on all levels. Actually I can't wait for them to go now that I think about it. It's gonna be time to celebrate.

Dad comes home later that evening and hearing the news, he's ecstatic, beaming and happy for me, and undeniably relieved. But, despite his relief and joy, he can't resist getting in a few shots about Ohio State – the "football school" – hardly Ivy League. I think he wants one of his sons to go to an Ivy League school. He wasn't able to, not because of his grades, but rather because of his age and when he graduated. He graduated at age 16, not entirely uncommon for his era, the late '20s. But he also graduated in January of his senior year. He would have gone to Penn, but instead ended up at Temple University, where he graduated at age 20 in 1931 then onto medical school back in New York. I guess he felt cheated and didn't want that to happen to his sons. First Dave, a very good student and a hard worker, gets rejected at Brown, Penn and Cornell and "settled" for Wisconsin.

Now four years later, me, a much poorer student, has no shot at the Ivy League, but at least I get into a Big Ten school. OSU is the first school I hear from and now that I am in, I can wait to hear from the remaining schools with a high degree of relaxation. I am still waiting to hear from Carnegie Tech, Cincinnati, University of Colorado and University of Wisconsin. I actually want to go to Wisconsin, mostly for its liberal/radical political reputation but also because I'd been there, staying with Dave, and I really liked it. It's becoming known as the Berkeley of the Midwest. Very political, very hip.

The next day, I hug my parents goodbye as they head into their taxicab, en route to Kennedy and then to Tucson. I feel happy for them. It's a good moment in our family's life. All is well, all healthy, all thriving. We even starting to get along, enjoying each other.

Anyway, on Wednesday, January 4, 1968, college-bound, I leave for school with the knowledge that my parents are out of town.

My brother Lew and housekeeper Zee will be at home with me. Dave, back in school in Madison is starting the last semester of his senior year. So, just the three of us. I am excited and filled with anticipation.

That afternoon after school, I invite my boys over for a game of poker. Quarter, half-dollar, the betting stakes. Six of my poker mates, Mark, Mac, Rob, Skip and David show. It's awesome fun. I win big. Thirty bucks. A lot of money. I have the feeling that I am breaking out of the pack. My focus is there. Usually a middling poker player, I suddenly have confidence to spare. I'm seeing the cards, reading the players. Picking up the cues. Anticipating. My friends, especially Skip, are dazed and dazzled. Skip, used to being the big winner, doesn't like it a bit. But he also, characteristically, makes room for it with caustic sardonic commentary as if he is the Yankee announcer, Mel Allen calling the game.

That night, brother Lew and I hang out listening to the underground FM station WOR playing their countdown of the top 400 rock songs of all time. I'm writing them down and when distracted by something else, enlist Lew to do it for me. He happily complies. Nice kid.

The next day, Mac, Mark and I drive to Cue Lounge, the local pool hall and play pool after school. Then it is onto Yonkers Raceway in the freezing cold for the harness racing winter season opener. I bet a bundle on Yankee Mick, a horse I've been following and betting on for a few months now. I bet on him to place. He comes in third. Not everything is going my way. Not just yet. I lose forty dollars.

Mac and Mark drop twenty-five. We don't care. It's the opener at YR. And as our old degenerate friend and mentor Sol once said about opening night, "You have to be there because everybody who is nobody is going to be there." He was right. We watch the races inside on TV at the YR as the ten degree weather that night makes it impossible to be outside on the blacktop, the area where we usually like to watch the races.

Mac is at the wheel of his father's 404 black Peugeot with the stick off the column as we drive home. He wonders who I'm going with to Becky's party that Friday night. I tell him I'm taking Jean O' Bannion. He is mildly surprised, temporarily forgetting that Marla and I broke up the previous week. Mark is going with Becky, his on again off again girlfriend. Mark plays the field when he plays at all. Mac's with Sue, his girlfriend of one year.

Friday, January 6, 1968, the night is clear, black, 30 degrees. I drive to pick up Jean O'Bannion in south New Rochelle. Driving back to the north end to Becky's house, we make out at every stop light as this is now our pattern. It's intense. French kiss lust between us. Getting to Becky's, we see that it is quite a small gathering, maybe five couples, harkening back to seventh grade make out parties. Inside, we pass a joint among the three couples, generational peace pipe ritual to the Doors' "Strange Days" and Beatles' "Magical Mystery Tour" albums. "People are Strange" holds a secret meaning when you are enthralled brain-wise by the enchantment of Acapulco Gold. Smacking my tongue against roof and teeth, mouth drying with sly laughter, horn doggery/cattery, now adjourning the group smoke and musicathon. Off into separate bedrooms, silent departings "While Suzanne holds the key," braying from Leonard Cohen's wail. Jean and I deep in enthrall, to first, then second in "no seconds" flat. Leading off second, thighs touching, hand sliding upstream, towards low middle with light turning green. Touching the cotton crunch of crackle sounds inside smells of smoke, incense, scent of sweat so sweet, brain going starkers with needy insurgency. Cotton, half-mast dungarees to knees, underpants pulled to knees as well. Wool mini skirt, folding on stomach and then... off with the lights. Get under the covers. Shirts unbuttoned from belly button down, males and females, Jean O'Bannion and me. And then more Leonard Cohen from the other room. "Oh, the sisters of mercy, they are not departed or gone."

Digit handles, simultaneous circular movements, once by Jean in and out around me. We're having some fun now. I yelp. Jean giggles then licks my ears like a cocker spaniel. Surrender – third base, nobody out.

"When the music's over – turn out the light."

Prep work is done. Prepare for entry. Turntable drops new record.

"Roll up – rollup for the mystery tour roll up, and that's an invitation."

Wetness abounding. Mounting a heat seeking missile, seeks juice bar cave for beetle nut encounter. Oh yeah. "Let's all get up and dance to a song that was a hit before your mother was born." Song four, side one "Magical Mystery Tour. " Coitus, proceeding? This time? The youth motto replaying again.

Mac is knocking on the door in his underpants, looking for a J. The schmuck.

And I'm wasted. We're all a little toasty now. Who knows what's being said, much less what is being heard. You know what? I didn't much care. I feel so mellow, peaceful. "Sex is sure better than anything except maybe baseball and rock 'n' roll. Although, it's close." I say to Mac, lying with a straight face.

The six of us reconnoiter and order pizza to accommodate our munchy mania. We call it a night early at midnight. We all got what we came for, sorta-kinda. I drop Jean O'Bannion off and go home. I sleeping fitfully for two hours.

January 7, '68. Brother Lew, our housekeeper Zee and I stay inside. The temperature dips to five degrees, with the wind chill factor, minus six. Snow looming. Lew and I watch six straight hours of sports and movies. Deadly, bed by 10. Dissipated. Lackluster.

January 8, 1968, Sunday. Sleep till noon. Wake up with head pounding from heater. Cotton mouthed. Pop a cigarette and search for brother Lew. He's already watching the tube. I eat one of Zee's patented bacon and egg breakfasts, with rye toast, medium bacon, coffee – instant Sanka. Another freezing January day to look forward to. Bored. Lew and I play ping pong, box and watch T.V., listening to four of the top 400 of all time on the radio. Writing it down. It's strange. I feel a weird feeling of clarity and exhilaration like never before. Pussy must be good for what ails you. Sure feels good. The day passes and Lew and I schmooze with Zee and watch the "Sand Pebbles" on TV. Hit the sack. School tomorrow.

Monday, January 9, 1968, Mac and I hook up at noon after class. We drive straight to the pool hall for four straight hours of eight ball and nine ball. Then after heading home and doing an hour's worth of homework, it's off again with Mac and Mark, this time in Mark's dad's Oldsmobile to Yonkers Raceway. Again, the weather sucks. It's freezing cold, forcing us once again inside to watch the races on T.V. This time we get shut out of all five races. I bet on Yankee Mick again, my favorite horse, only this time to win. He places. Damn, I keep missing on this fucking horse. Next time he's gonna come in.

Mac and Mark and I reassure ourselves, betraying some doubt in our voices. We arrive home at ten that night. I can't sleep. I make my top 40 list of all time rock 'n' roll songs. Then, still not tired I make my list of top 40 movies of all time. Then I make my list of top 10 girls of all time. The latter utilizes five criteria: looks, sexiness, niceness, brains and athleticism. Surprisingly, neither Jean O'Bannion nor Greta, not even Marla finish first, but rather Mac's girlfriend, Sue. Sue and I went steady in eighth grade for a month, non-French kissing, and she remained a good friend. I ask Mac the next day how he feels about sharing the wealth or playing switchies. Surprisingly, he doesn't mind. He'd always had a hankering for Marla anyway. I tell him, I'd suspected that and we kind of laugh over the idea of changing partners. The same afternoon, I run into Marla for the first time since she surprised me that New Year's Eve night. It doesn't take long, and now we're going steady again. Believe it or not, this is the fourth time we're going steady. We've only been together fifteen months and already we've had three break ups. All initiated by me. It seems we can't stay apart. I don't tell her about Sue's pending visit to my house that afternoon. Who needs the hassle?

It's amazing enough that Mac gives me the green light for a one shot deal. Neither of us speak to our girlfriends about it. We aren't really good at communicating our needs and desires to them. Nor do we, I suspect, think that they are going to go along with the scheme, if we ask. So, it's just easier to act as if Sue's visit to my house is an innocent event, vice versa Mac's invitation to have Marla come over. Sue comes over at 4:00 p.m. We talk great together. Like brother and sister. We laugh a lot. We get deep and honest about family, parents, girlfriends, boyfriends, school, future plans. And we talk about the larger issues, too. Race, politics, drugs, even philosophy and religion. She's smart, soon to be a freshman at Goucher College in Maryland. A brunette beauty. Sweet, with a good body. We kiss. Get into it. Sue doesn't mind. She tells me that she loves me and always did and said she can easily be with me if she and Mac don't make it.

I nod and share that I don't think Marla and I have much in common other than having fun together, dancing and listening to music. I guess I like being loved by someone in love with me. Sue asked how I feel. Fledgling therapist that she is. Perplexed, I don't really know. Confused, but exhilarated by all the attention I am getting from all kinds of women the past few weeks. We dry hump.

I tell her we should get married someday because we get along so well. She agrees. We hug. She leaves and I feel a warm glow. Number One of all time. "Of all tiiiime," as Ali would say it.

That night, no track, no girls, no homework, no TV, no music. I just read my parents' books. Modern classic hard covers. Madly searching for answers. I'm suddenly philosophical. Nietzsche, Freud, Marx, Plato, Camus and Hemingway. I don't really read these books, mind you. I scan the table of contents and make another list. What is the meaning of life? The top ten in descending order is ten: *Friendship*; nine: *Freedom*; eight: *Fun*; seven: *Sex*; six: *Peace*; five: *Beauty*; four: *Justice*; three: *Goodness*; two: *Truth*; one: *Love*.

I can't decide. It comes down to the last two. In this corner, LOVE, in the red trunks from Venus, California. And in the other corner, in the black trunks, from Buffalo, New York TRUTH. For the heavyweight, intellectual title fight of the millennium. Winner becomes the MEANING OF LIFE. For me, for everyone. Individual answer – collective answer. From midnight to 5:00 am, I jab, punch, mull back and forth between the two. Actually, pacing back and forth is more like it.

Finally, after consuming four packs of cigarettes, exhausted, overtired, wasted, I look into the bathroom mirror to see an unshaven, gaunt, angular, peaked looking face. Getting on the scale, I am shocked to see I've lost fifteen pounds in seven days. Down to one thirty. No big deal, I think as I light up another Marlboro. I make my announcement in two hours.

Wednesday, January 11, 7:30 a.m. Mr. Levy's Problems of American Democracy. I'm the first one in. Revved, expectant. I sit at the edge of my seat as the class files in. With his usual lackadaisical manner, Levy comes in last, his magnificent shock of white hair, and a tan fresh from a week in Puerto Rico. Suddenly standing up, without raising my hand I blurt out to Levy before he sits in his chair amongst the students in a circle.

"I need to address the class." He says sure, but I am already heading to the front of the room without waiting for an answer.

Levy asks, "Is everything all right?" I nod my head and proceed with my statement.

"I need to make an announcement," I say. "I just want to let you all know that you've all had me wrong all these years. I am not what I appear. I am a big fake. I lie, I cheat on tests, I steal money from my parents, I smoke dope, I cut school and I'm a virgin."

I go on for another ten minutes listing every transgression I've ever committed, stealing, cheating, nasty comments to people, backbiting, every possible "sin" that comes to mind. Speed rapping, frenetic, pacing and rapping at the same time, I notice a sea of hands raised as I go on. I stop and ask for questions. First, there is a stunned silence. Then, I call on some hands. The students themselves seem moved by this verbal avalanche and upon calling on them to speak or ask questions they seem to go onto their own version of confession about their lives. Some are teary-eyed. Many, clearly shaken up. After three or four females as well as males speak with their own revelations, Levy asks me how I've come to these revelations of mine. I reply, "From staying up all night." I then say, "I am leaving now," and walk out of class.

Cool, confident and cocky. I know the answer. I can feel it. They know, too. They know I know. Walking down to the lobby, facing the parking lot of the high school, I suddenly feel exhausted. Without thinking about the fact that I am at my high school, I lie down under a table and stretch out while students and teachers come and go. Strangely, no one says a word to me for a while, until Sue, with a hall pass, pats me on the shoulder.

"Are you all right, Arnie?"

"Yeah," I say blasé like.

"What are you doing lying down?"

"I'm tired," I reply blankly.

Sue: "Do you feel ok?"

Me: "Yeah, I feel great. I'm dynamite."

Sue: "What?"

"I'm dynamite and I'm happening," I say. And with that, sensing that she doesn't get what I am saying, I impatiently stand up and head out the door. I light up a Marlboro at the top step and I see a mate of mine from the football team, smoking a Marlboro as well. I light into him immediately about his "phony" ways. He looks at me funny-like, his mouth dropped open in shock, stunned. And it keeps happening with every conversation. There are plenty of conversations... boom, boom, boom, one after another. In every one of them I tell them exactly what I think of them. Usually the stuff they don't want to hear. Straight. THE TRUTH. Not just as I see it but how it IS. "Enough of this crap," I think and say.

I know the MEANING OF LIFE. That's how it is – period. And if they can't handle it, they better get onto themselves. I'm not holding back. After about ten minutes of this, bombarding acquaintances and friends alike, I split.

In my car now, the exhilaration is really surging. I'm thinking I'm gonna be famous. I'm gonna be interviewed as the seventeen-year-old kid who has discovered the meaning of life. Getting into my Falcon, I turn on the radio, expecting Huntley and Brinkley to announce my discovery. I think if I've discovered the meaning of life, then I must be JESUS. Whoo, I'm powerful... Whoa... Wait a minute. If I'm God or Jesus, then I'm dead. I'm gonna be killed. Terror, shockwaves go through me for the first time in weeks. I'm gonna be killed. Mafia for sure. Wait a minute. Weren't those guys I talked to on the steps today connected? I'm dead.

Fear-struck, I race home and zoom out of the car into my house. Close the door. Pull the drapes across the living room window. PANIC. Thoughts racing. Pacing feet. Agitated. I can't get my bearings. I'm scared. They're gonna kill me. Don't go near that window. Stay away. I'm muttering out loud now. Zee comes up from downstairs where she's been ironing.

"Arnie. Is that you? What's happening?"

"Nothing – nigger." I hear the word jump off my tongue. She slams the door and goes back downstairs to the basement. I think I hear, "I quit. I don't need this bullshit."

Oh no. Now I've done it. What am I gonna do now? I don't know what to do. I'm beside myself. For some reason, I remember I have a shrink appointment at 2:00 and momentarily that centers me.

Then the floodgates open. Sobbing uncontrollably, I alternate between tears and fears of a homicidal attack. Terrified, I stay like this for five hours. One minute sobbing, the next angry, the next sexual limerence, smoking pacing up and down. I drive to Dr. Chidas in Scarsdale. I must be in a daze, because I can't recall the drive at all, but when I get into Chidas's office, he takes one look at me and says that I'm manicky. He says he's gonna put me on Thorazine which I refuse. He asks about drugs. I say, "Pot. That's all." He says, "Are you sure?" I say, "Yeah." He asks if I can drive home and I say I can. He asks about the parents and I tell him they're in Arizona, but I'll call them.

I leave his office, drive home and crash for hours. Waking up, feeling speedy, I call up the folks in Arizona before midnight, not able to go to sleep. I reiterate my confessional list to them that I recited in Levy's class. I tell them that I love them, probably unbegrudgingly for the first time in years. They are alarmed and tell me they're coming home on the next plane tomorrow but I ask them not to. They say I need them, and that they are coming home. I rage after I get off the phone.

Next day, I don't go to school but see Chidas again. He gives me Thorazine. This time, I take it and he drives me home. My parents arrive two hours later. I'm beside myself. Frantic, panicked and paranoid and definitely not looking forward to my parents' return.

Not looking forward to seeing my father, especially. I know what he'll do, I think to myself, he'll grill me, get upset, get pushy, try to find out what is going on and fix it. Fuck him. If he wants a fight, I'll give him a fight. Cocksucker, fuck him. Zee and Lew are here at home with me, worried. They don't know what to do. I'm pacing around like a caged Bengal tiger: unshaven, unkempt, chain-smoking, not eating. Now, I got this tranq in my system. Great! 100 mg. of Thorazine four times a day. Yeah, lot of good that'll do.

A car pulls up and I hear doors slamming. Oh shit. My stomach shutters. Oh fuck. Dread fills me. Here they come! Click clack of heels up the three steps leading to the front door. Then the pitter patter of dad's shoes and the taxi driver leaving suitcases on the steps and being shoed away by Dad. The doorbell ringing. I answer the open glass enclosed screen door.

"Arnie," my mother half shrieks as she moves forward to embrace me in relieved fright.

"Don't come near me, unless you want to fight," I say backpedalling and half-mockingly putting up my dukes.

"I'm not here to fight, Arn. I'm here to get you well."

"Yeah right," I say with disbelieving fear/anger, still keeping my distance. "Stay the fuck away from me."

"Okay, Arnie," Mom intones. "What's going on here? What's wrong? You look so thin, what's the matter?"

"Fuck off, just fuck off. Both of you. Fuck off. I hate you both. You too, Ma. Leave me the fuck alone. Let me be. I'll be all right.

Mom: "Let's you and me go upstairs, get unpacked and we'll have some tea. It'll be relaxing. Okay?"

"Yeah," I say in a suddenly changed tone.

"That's better."

"I don't want any questions Dad, you hear? No fucking questions. I'll talk when I'm ready and not before. Get me?" I'm wired, tired, geared for battle, weary at the same time.

Dad and Mom look beat, too. I suddenly feel bad for them. Bad for Zee and Lew, too. They don't need this. Nobody needs this. This sucks. I agree. There are two people inside of me, talking. The me who has feelings and the me overseeing the events trying to stay calm, rational and in control. That part is starting to feel guilty, weary, depressed and sad now. But I'm still pretty alert to the ever-present danger of a verbal assault from my father, the ace clinical investigator, non-pareil. He always gets his man (makes the differential diagnosis). That's why they pay him the big bucks. "Vee have vays to make you talk." I'll be damned, just like the longshoreman on the docks. I don't know nothing. D and D (Deaf and Dumb).

After five minutes, they're back in house clothes, clearly exhausted. They make small talk and we drink Earl Grey together. I'm agitated. They're worried and alarmed. Not prepared for the sight that is me. It's not a pretty picture. Currier and Ives would not be making pictures of this family tonight. Edvard Munch would. I'm pacing. Starting to feel some strange sensations never before felt. Thorazine, probably.

"I need to go to my room," I hear myself saying. I split without waiting for a reply and I collapse on my back, flat, petrified. After a little while, dad comes in and asks, "Are you all right?"

"Yeah," I mumble, not wanting to impose or have my father involved with this. The fucking jerk, I'll handle this alone, thank you. He leaves. Now I'm panicking. Oh shit. I can't get my bearings. I feel weird. I can't gather my thoughts. I don't feel like myself. I'm freaking. I can't handle this. I'm on the bed and try to lay there. But I'm up. I light a cigarette. I can't focus. I can't think. Pacing. Try to lie down, I tell myself. Can't. Sit up, thoughts racing faster and faster. Really frightened now. Feeling terrified. It's the end. I feel like screaming but I can't. I'm coming apart at the seams.

"Don't move," the thought comes up out of some unknown chamber somewhere in me. I don't move. "Try to stay still, " I doctor myself, a la Ingrid Bergman playing the psychoanalyst in Hitchcock's "Spellbound." "Try to relax. Let the medicine work on you. You'll be all right. You need sleep." I close my eyes. "You'll feel better. You need rest, Arnie."

I open my eyes. It's Mom. She's been there for a while talking to me while my eyes were closed. I mistook her voice for my own recollection of Ingrid Bergman's voice. I feel relieved. My mother's voice is soothing.

"Hi Mom," I murmur.

"Hi pussycat," she answers.

"Feeling better?"

"Yeah." This time for real. "Yeah, I'm okay."

"Get some sleep, sweetie pie and we'll talk in the morning."
I collapse into unconsciousness for twelve hours.

CHAPTER 28

Jesus Christ: A Close Personal Friend of Mine

I don't go to school, obviously. Sleep till 10:00 a.m. Wake up groggy, cotton-mouthed. Feeling a little better but as I get up, I feel dizzy. Orthostatic hypotension. Who knew? It scares the shit out of me. I think I'm gonna pass out. I don't but slowly rise, straightening out and hesitantly make my way down the three steps from my bedroom, past the foyer into the kitchen where Zee has made bacon, eggs, toast and jam. It feels good to eat. Dad has gone to work. He's in Manhattan, making rounds, believe it or not. Mom is there. I can't talk. I am still very agitated. Hyper-suspicious. A visit to Dr. Chidas' office has been scheduled: Mom and me, Scarsdale at 11:30 a.m.

After scarfing down Zee's fabulous (as always) breakfast, we drive over to Chidas' in Mom's gold '67 Pontiac Tempest, black vinyl top. The trip, mostly in silence, with Ma occasionally glancing over at me with a concerned look which masks deep worry. Not too hard to discern, even by the likes of this psychotic reporter. Clearly, she's trying to communicate some degree of calm, but she can't help but telegraph alarm. At first it angers me, but worse, it scares me, making me feel like I'm an alien weirdo. My own mother – helpless, panic stricken, worried. I can't take this, my defenses are shot, gone. Her facial expressions go right to my limbic circuit box filling me with shock waves of electric currents adding to my sensation of out of controlness.

Ah, the woman can't help it. She's out of her depth. Her sonny boy is flipping out and she really doesn't know what to do. Doesn't really know how to be. I certainly can't help her. I am too malleable and susceptible to external vibrations. Any sense of environmental pull that is at all negative and I react immediately, intensely, with little restraint or modulation. I can't help it. That's where I am. "Labile," is what the shrinks call it. "Volatile, livewire," is what I call it.

Chidas does his best to calm my mom down, to put what's happening to me in some kind of context – for her. Identity crisis, father complex, inferiority complex, some of the lingo being thrown around. I am using the generational rhetoric of my peers and times. The combination ghetto slang/drug culture/hippie/beat argot. The communication is strained. I am groggy from the Thorazine, now taking effect, but the next minute, jumping at anything that triggers my sense of being misunderstood, particularly by the shrink.

He recommends I stay out of school until I felt better. Stabilize and regroup. Get rest and nourishment, the whole "geshichta." We leave and go to a kosher deli. I have a corned beef sandwich, vanilla malted and head back to New Rochelle. My mom's plan is to fatten me up so milkshakes are clearly on the bill of fare.

On the ride home, she listens to her station that plays a lot of Sinatra and Bing Crosby and I am strangely comforted by the music. Music I usually find mostly boring, being restless for my rock 'n' roll. Back home, I put on Richie Havens' "Mixed Bag." Lying down on the couch, I get sad, and cry and finally fall asleep for a couple of hours.

I hear the sound of the electric garage door and my father's Peugeot disturbing my dream and waking me. It's 4:00 in the afternoon on Friday and Dad is back from the city after seeing patients, doing his rounds at his three hospitals, whatever. As he arrives in the house, I'm thinking I am asleep. I overhear him whispering to Mom about me.

"How is he? What did Chidas say? Did he tell you much?" Blah, blah, blah. It makes me paranoid and I don't need much help in this department. I can assure you. It jangles my already frayed equilibrium, and downshifts me a notch into panic/dread, disorientation mode. I remain on the couch, faking sleep for two more hours until dinner.

Then Zee wakes me for our usual Friday night brisket dinner. My mother's brisket tastes good, no matter how psychotic you are and tonight is no exception. This is the only good thing. My father, fresh from his patient attending, is loaded for bear.

And the clinical interrogation begins. At first slowly, through dinner and dessert, with a break for Knick basketball on T.V. Then commencing again at 10:00 p.m., when I can't sleep or stay still. "Akathesia," they call it. "Ants in your pants and need to dance," I call it. Pacing, edgy. Mom, Lew, Zee make their exits to their respective quarters for the evening. Lew, to his room across from mine, Mom, to hers a bit down the hall, and Zee downstairs to hers, formerly brother Dave's room. Only Dad and I remain.

We're in the kitchen now together. Me, smoking my Viceroys, my alternate brand, Dad chaining the Chuckles left out on the table. The ole sweet tooth. One of my dad's many weaknesses.

He is clearly daunted, perplexed, upset. He's just not used to not knowing what is happening, particularly in *clinical* situations. And this is clearly a clinical situation. The fact that it is a father-son scenario only adds to the complexity, but does not alter the objective for my diagnostician doctor dad. An answer must be found. Why is Arnie psychotic? How could we have left a healthy, seventeen-year-old ten days ago and returned to find a wild, crazy, paranoid, hyped up, hyperkinetic volatile kid?

I am not a helpful subject. Not because I don't want to be, which I don't, but because I don't know myself. I also am not particularly interested in that question right now. Terrified half the time, I am deeply mistrustful of my father. He isn't really interested in understanding what's going on with me, but rather in reducing, boiling it down. I need concern, empathy, understanding, someone caring, not cause and effect explanations or inquiries. Our interests are at loggerheads. We are, in the parlance of the times, in "two different places."

The interview proceeds. Dad has an hypothesis: LSD. Either I dropped it or it was slipped into a drink. "Mickey Finn," he calls it. I don't think so. I have more faith in my brethren than he does. Generations colliding. The discussion makes me nervous, worried, more scattered and angrier. It's a harangue. This is for him. His curiosity needs sating. My wellbeing is secondary. A doctor first or rather a scientist, a diagnostician first and a father second. A concerned, compassionate, caring human third. He knows little about that at least when it comes to how he relates to me. Knowledge, that is what comes first. Science and knowledge, they count. He can't connect. I need him to connect. I need it from his entire fucking generation. Finding it is rare. My mother, while more caring, is not really equipped to understand what is happening in any meaningful way. She's too overwhelmed, I guess. It's ludicrous, how deep and wide the gap is between them and me.

The interview/interrogation goes on for four fucking hours. Viceroy after Viceroy, moving from kitchen to living room and back again. By 2:00 a.m. I am exhausted. I'm agitated, nervous, disorganized, scared and intermittently feeling somewhat zombie-like. I make a knife-life gesture with my hand, finally to signal no mas.

We are lost in some sort of obsessional no man's land for the last hour or so, with a dead-end neurotic interactional cycle that I am clearly bearing the brunt of. My father may be confused, perplexed, even guilt-ridden for that matter, but I am sliding into annihilation anxiety, once again feeling like I am coming apart, disappearing into space.

Adieu Dad. I'm going to my bed. Now on top of the covers, prone position. The ceiling is spinning. I'm sweating. Dissolving. Falling through the cracks. Into space, veering into a black hole. I'm dying. THIS IS IT! I'm not gonna be alive tomorrow. I know it. I'm panicking. I'm gone. Help me. I can't yell out, interiorized, out of touch with reality, helpless, alone. Isolated. Caught in an interior world of weird images, converging, back and forth. Sensations of shrapnel, hitting up against thoughts, splintering, grasping for the seam, fresh out of solutions. Spinning, falling into praying now.

"Please, Jesus, if you let me live, I'll do anything you ask. Just let me live to see tomorrow." Unspeakable terror, I'm fighting for dear life, fighting/frightening, making it worse, vice grip, fight, tight, fright, dying, grabbing fighting, strangling, gasping now. Can't catch my breath, throat tightening cobra around my neck, inside my neck. Can't breathe! Die sucker die, die and die. Give up, give up, give up, give up, give up. You lose. Surrounded... you die. You're dead!

CHAPTER 29

The Infinity Limited

CHIRP, CHIRP, CHIRP. Sparrows. The glint of light through my skull penetrating the cavity in the wires where synaptic firings light a fuse and open like a vagina making room for a laser penis. Only it's the sunlight piercing my unconscious Thorazine-soaked, psychotic acid-laced brain, waking me up, opening my eyes. I AM ALIVE. Thank you, Lord. Thank you, Jesus. I live to fight another day. Eecch. Genuflect, breathe, release of energy through sigh of relief, stick out arm in black power salute. "Oh baby," I hear myself say through Thorazine dream-haze, as waking begins. I am alive. I am alive. Whewwww. Not so fast, my body announces as I sit up from bed. Immediate nausea and dizziness. Zee's voice outside. Then a knock, door opens. "Arnie, are you up, man? I got breakfast. You ready?"

Me: "Thanks. Yup. Food?"

Zee: "Yes, bacon and eggs, toast, coffee."

Me: "Be right down."

I haltingly stumble down the stairs into the kitchen, park myself at the head of the table and slowly take the food in, until my stomach sends the signal it's okay and now I can eat with my usual haste. The eggs and toast taste good washed down with orange juice and a spot of coffee. But as always, the bacon hits the spot. Now done. I breathe a sigh of relief. Light up a Viceroy. Yes, life goes on.

Once again, Dad is in New York making rounds. Mom is downstairs, the ghost, chain-smoking Larks, talking to me as I eat breakfast. "How are you? I've been so worried about you! How did you sleep?" she asks, scrambled all at once.

"I feel okay. I survived," I say.

"Survived? What do you mean?"

"Ma, I almost died last night."

"What?" Mom is in shock.

"I nearly died last night, but Jesus saved me," I say in a tone of grateful relief.

"Oh, Arnie, you poor thing," Mom murmurs in alarm, lighting up still another Lark.

"You don't get it, Ma. I'm born again. I died last night. I don't think you heard me," now shouting, "I died last night. But I'm saved now."

"Oh God, well let's wait till we talk to Dr. Chidas this morning. How are you feeling, pussycat?" she continues in disbelief and concern.

"Unbelievable," I come back with. "It's like a whole new world. Everything is new, fresh. That sunshine is so nice. God, it's great to be alive."

Mom: "Yeah, you know I'm glad you're feeling better. It's important that you eat though. You look so gaunt and thin. I'm gonna fatten you up with plenty of milkshakes."

This made me feel bad but nice, too.

"Thanks, Ma," I muster in reply.

Some semblance of normalcy is returning between us as we share a cigarette, as if we are Ann Sheridan and John Garfield in "They Made Me a Criminal." My mother reminds me of Lauren Bacall, in her low timbre, but she smokes like Bette Davis. Blows the smoke off the end of her lips, like a weird exhaust pipe. "A classy dame," my dad would say. I thought so too, except for the fact that she was my mother. Dressed right out of Bonwit Teller and Lord and Taylor. We finish our cigarettes and then Mom retreats to her room. I retreat to the den to begin my rest, relaxation and recovery. The recuperation from what I guess is nervous exhaustion or a nervous breakdown commences.

I stay home for about a week, going to my shrink appointments about three times a week and continuing on a relatively low dose of Thorazine, 100 mg. My sleep pattern returns. Zee and my mother fattened me up on milk shakes, scrambled eggs and healthy installments of spaghetti. In no time, I gain back ten of the fifteen pounds that I lost. Back up to my former welterweight class, 140 pounds. Clean-shaven, able to read again. Less jumpy. Less agitated.

I regain my capacity to stay on subject in conversation. I am again able to listen when people are talking to me without changing the subject or misapprehending what they are trying to say. In short, I start slowing down enough to get back on the conventional wavelength.

After a weeklong recovery period, Chidas and my parents agree with me that it might be worth a shot to try returning to high school. I missed the first week of the new semester, but the principal assures my parents that I can easily make it up. They encourage me to return and to take my time and take it easy.

January 29, Monday, I go back. Classes go smoothly the first couple of days. English class with Mrs. Schmuckler – check. Economics with Miss Margules – check. Psychology with Mr. Satcher – check plus. He's glad to have me back and is now starting a new unit on Personality, with an emphasis on Freud's theory of personality. Finally, Levy's Problems of American Democracy – check plus, here too as the class discusses the separation of Church and State written into the Constitution.

On Wednesday, January 31, in Mr. Satcher's class, my armor first begins to crack like the Liberty Bell as he begins his explication of Freud's theory of personality. First the topographic model: Unconscious, Preconscious and Conscious then the Structural model: Id, Ego, Superego. I start relating to the dynamics of the classroom in a highly symbolic, affectively charged way. Attributing every move of Satcher's speech, body language, tone and facial expressions as meaningful, not to mention the reactions of my fellow students to his lecture. I understand the meta-message or underlying meaning of what is going on. I see it as all directed at me, and not only that but that I am the author of what is coming out of Satcher's mouth and the students' responses. It's as if I know what is going to happen before it happens. I'm in touch with everybody's psychological problems and how they interact with Satcher's issues and role as a teacher and how this plays out in the conversational back and forth. I feel it, know it, predict it and am intensely involved in it on this level. It's intense. I feel like I'm communicating with Satcher, or rather the experience is that I'm meta-communicating. Ironically, knowingly, with laughter, my responses are completely inappropriate to the topic at hand, that is, objectively. The rest of the class is perplexed, disturbed and annoyed by my behavior, at least the ones who are not asleep, which are not many. Satcher knows that something is wrong. He has heard about my previous bout of weirdness and is alert for it. Besides, this is a psychology class. He knows something about psychology.

Also, he knows something about me. I seem manicky again and he says this aloud in class, addressing me. He speaks to me after class and tells me to go home because he thinks I'm getting over stimulated. He thinks that I'm not filtering adequately. He's right. Damn it. It's upsetting. So, I take his advice, cut the rest of my classes, get in my Peugeot 403 and head home, defeated.

That afternoon, beaten down, I see the shrink. He has my mother come in and we discuss a new plan for the first time. The Institute of Living. A residential place. A hospital, where I can go to school, graduate high school, do little, play sports and get better. A fancy nuthouse, in short. I balk. My mother balks. I suggest living somewhere else, instead of home. Maybe the atmosphere at home is too charged. Clearly, meaning my stupid father the "bulvan", the Sherman tank who stirs me up and sets me off. But Chidas doesn't think so. He thinks I need to go to "sleep-away camp." He thinks I need to be out of the home, out of the town, out of the school. Away. While we're in the office, he calls Hartford and sets up an appointment to go visit the place in two days.

In a few days, I go to see it, meet with social workers, who interview me and show me around the place. Big, with lots of grassy land and a campus to walk around in. It's decided a couple of days later. Chidas is adamant that this is the right decision. My parents, particularly my mom, slowly capitulate. Dad signs on sooner. He buys into the psychiatrist's rationale, which on the face of it is sound.

So, now it's all over but the shouting. Soon it will be goodbye Daisy Farms Drive, home of my parents, place of my childhood. Goodbye New Rochelle High, my high school. Goodbye to my three best friends, Mac, Mark and Rick. Goodbye Greta, beat girl nonpareil. Goodbye Jean O'Bannion, my wild Irish rose. Goodbye Becky, sometime girlfriend to Mark. Goodbye Sue, girlfriend to Mac, and number one on my all-time list of girlfriends. Goodbye Marla, first love of my life, current girlfriend and mostly faithful companion. Goodbye childhood. Parents, goodbye. Center field, senior year varsity baseball, starting spot, batting second, goodbye.

This was what is left. Goodbye. Goodbye would be said fluidly, stolidly, methodically.

I'm leaving. All of my friends come to the house to bid me adieu. Finally, only three and a girlfriend are left at the end. Mark, Rick – Tennis foe Rick – and Marla. They come over on my last night, Valentine's Day, to say their farewells.

Mark, loose, casual, relaxed betraying no concern for my future. Rick, very concerned, encouraging, emphasizing the need to fortify myself with good music (Beatles records especially), books (Salinger, Dostoevsky, *Moby Dick* and, last and most important, *Heller's Catch 22*) and movies (Bogart films, Paul Newman films, Brando films). Mark and Rick both stress that they will visit soon and often. Then they leave. First, Mark and ten minutes later, Rick. Now it's 9:00 p.m. The doorbell rings. Marla, the cutie pie, appears at the door with jeans and her trademark turtleneck doing a very good impression of upbeat. This doesn't last. Before too long she's crying. Trying to be reassuring, she requires a lot of hugging, comfort and reassurance from me. It's kind of unbearable for me seeing her in so much pain. She really loves me. I can feel it and am overtaken by immense sadness for her and me. She has been shell-shocked by my illness, matured way past what any seventeen-year-old, nice Jewish girl from a nice Jewish family should have to go through. No sarcasm here. At all. Just sad. Sad going through it and sad having to recall it. We hold each other – tight. Few words are spoken by the end. I can't take it. I can't handle the depth and power of feeling. Her heartbreak, mine, the heartbreak of the heartbreaking situation.

It's all way too much. Despite her tears, she's really a trooper and recovers nicely and is ultimately really there for me. I smile grimly at the end. She promises to call, write and visit soon. Such loyalty, fidelity, devotion and adoration. I am eternally grateful. I probably never told her so. We never talked about it afterward. Frankly, there was too much hurt and anger in what came later, but this was a long time ago, now fifty years ago, 1968. Life is funny. You don't get second chances. That night, Valentine's Day, was the closest we ever were.

Marla hugs me, kisses me, tenderly. We touch fingers lightly. Walking out into the cold snowy February night, I watch as she disappears into her light blue Chevy Impala. With one last glance, our eyes lock. She gives me a deep smile of recognition, of love and loss and backs out of the driveway. I shut the front door and turn out the living room lights and trudge up the stairs. I turn on the radio, take my clothes off, leaving my underpants and tee shirt on, get under the covers and listen as Dr. Timothy Leary expounds on the *Politics of Ecstasy*, the psychedelic apocalypse on Barry Gray, on station W.M.C.A. I find Leary soothing and strangely hope-inducing.

Next day, my parents drive me up the New England Thruway, the two hours to Hartford, and deposit me in the lobby of the Hartford Retreat for the Insane. Henceforth, to be referred to as the IOL (Institute of Living).

END OF PART ONE

Part Two

CHAPTER 30

IOL: The Setting, The Players

I don't recall much of that first day other than the perfunctory tour conducted by the social worker. The school, the social area, the art facilities (art works, leather works, ceramics), the grounds and the unit. What I remember most vividly is Ms. Gray walking me into the social area where the patients spend the bulk of their time. Activities here are, for the most part voluntary, though I didn't know it at the time, in contrast in many long-term hospitals, activities are mostly compulsory. So, where I am the bulk of the inmates wile away hours of each day hanging out, being anxious or spaced out or playing cards. I am, to say the least, not prepared for what I'm seeing.

All manner of weirdness awaits me here at the Lounge, our name for the social area. I immediately search for my peer group – anyone my own age. There they are by the ice cream parlor. There are about eight or nine that day, and they eye me critically. I must have the same look they see in all the new inmates, frightened and bewildered. That's how we all look in our orientation ride on the "getting-to-know-you parade", which is what they call it laughingly. I want to run. It is so defeating, humiliating, scary and weird, all at once. And, no doubt, I don't have the presence of mind to hide my feelings. Being crazy and not quite completely zombied out on Thorazine will do that. So, there I am, an exposed nerve in a nuthouse. Apt, I guess.

Sensing my discomfort, Ms. Grey whisks me through the Lounge back to my unit, Butler I, where she introduces me to the head nurse and then leaves. Miss Berra, a mostly genuine robin, exudes caring as she explains some of the rules and ways of the unit. Then she points me to my room. I can't get there fast enough. I dive onto the bed, one of two in the room, and cry my eyes out for an hour before falling asleep. Around 5:30 that evening, I wake up to the rustling of sounds and voices.

"Freeman, your new roommate is here. He's sleeping. Please don't wake him. He'll need your help and support to show him the ropes."

"Ok, Miss Berra," Freeman says breezily.

Freeman: "Ok, what's his name"?

Miss Berra: "Arnie. Arnie Brucher. From New York, somewhere. I think New Rochelle."

"Mm, wonder if he plays ball. Ok, Ms. Berra. I'll tune 'em in."

"Thanks, Freeman."

I'm awake now. Groggy eyes, matted with sleep gunk.

Freeman says jocularly but somewhat over the top, "Hey, what'd ya' say, man? My name's Freeman. I hear yours is Arnie. How ya' doin'?"

Me, a little hesitantly: "Mm, okay. I guess. Nice to meet you."

Freeman: "When d'ja get here?"

Me: "About noon today."

Freeman: "Ah, well... welcome aboard, I guess." He is cackling by the end of his greeting.

Me: "How long you been here?"

Freeman: "Mm... about six months. But I'll be leaving in a few months."

Me: "Mm, is that 'bout average?"

Freeman: "Ah, well... It depends. Some leave after four months and some stay two or three years. Depends."

Me: "Oh."

Freeman: "Don't worry man. You'll get out. It's the first question everybody asks when they get here. Just take it easy. You'll get out. What're you in for?"

Me: "Nervous breakdown."

Freeman: "Oh yeah. Me, too."

Me: "What happened to you?"

Freeman: "Flipped out I guess. Thought I was Jesus. Didn't sleep for three days. Fighting cops. Pretty nutso, huh? How 'bout you?"

Me: "The Christ thing. No sleep. Sounds pretty similar, I guess."

Freeman: "Weird, huh?"

Me: "Yeah. How do you feel now, Freeman?"

Freeman: "Better, I guess. Still get kind of depressed a lot, angry, scared some. I don't know. Wanting to get out. Feeling cooped up, that kind of thing. How 'bout you?"

Me: "Scared, down, worried. I don't know. I wanna get out soon. Whatever it takes. I really want to graduate with my high school back in New Rochelle and play ball for my high school varsity team. So, what does it take to get out of here?"

Freeman: "Your doctor's gotta think you're ready to leave. Don't ask me when they think you are. I think it's when they think you're in control of your emotions and can handle it out in the world, I guess."

Me sighing: "Oh... I guess it's gonna be awhile for me, I think."

Freeman: "Ah, don't sweat it. Hey, you play ball, huh? I thought I heard you say you want to play baseball for your high school. Is that right?"

Me nodding: "Yeah, a lot."

Freeman: "Any good?"

I nod.

Freeman: "Great. What position?"

Me: "Outfield, infield – either way. I can do both."

Freeman: "Cool. We're getting a team together. Milstein, Bufman and some other guys from the other unit, Fuller II. We're gonna take on Data Processing. Maybe some of the shrinks, too. Interested?"

Me: "Definitely. Let me know. It'll give us something to do, huh?"

Freeman: "Definitamente. Oh, right." Looking down at his watch, "It's time we head out to have dinner. Specialite de la maison today."

Me: "Yeah, what?"

Freeman: "Shit on a shingle."

Me: "Oh. Sounds great." It wasn't. It wasn't quite shit on a shingle but it was close. Chipped beef with cream sauce. More like puke on a plate.

After dinner, I'm sitting in an armchair in the foyer of the unit, smoking Viceroy after Viceroy, when two sleazy yet interesting characters, sort of hippyish in demeanor, slide by me, grinning knowingly to themselves. The one farthest from me, walking slightly ahead of the other guy, is more angular. While the other guy – Yip is his name – has a more rolly polly look. They remind me for some reason of characters out of *Huckleberry Finn*. I'm not proven wrong. They are American originals.

"Hey, uh... Yip. Looks like there's an... uh, new mute been brought into the festivities."

Yip: "Well, Foxy. I reckon you may be onto something here. I wonder what this particular mute is doing here? What's your best guess?"

Foxy: "I dunno, YPSL. By the looks of this guy, his blonde hair, anxious demeanor, rapid-fire-deep-inhalation-like behavior, I would guess he's your basic Nervous Breakdown- middleclass-Jewish kind of guy."

Yip: "Now, now my Foxy. Let's not be lazy here. Not be too quick to rush to judgment. You know what kind of trouble that can get you into. Need I remind you of your credit card work?"

Fox: "That's my Yip. You're right, Yip. I'm glad you're here to remind me of my hasty tendencies and the trouble that can ensue. I think we should saunter back and find out. You know, be empirical, scientific about this. What say?"

All this while the two of them are pacing up and down the unit's carpet-strewn hallway.

Yip, clucking his tongue: "Lead the way, mine Fox."

So the two of them make their way down the corridor towards me in my vinyl armchair entwined pretzel-like with my Viceroys.

Yip: "Attention, young man. Wherefore art thou young man? Hark. What are you doing here, young man?"

Me, shrugging my shoulders, shaking my head: "Huh. Oh... Mm..."

Yip: "Speak, young man. We are your goodwill ambassadors. Here to introduce you to life as we know it, as it is lived or practiced on this here unit, Butler I."

Me, laughing: "That's funny. Well. Okay." Haltingly, "My name is Arnie and I'm from New Rochelle..... New York."

Fox: "Oh, Hmm. Arnie, Arnie, Arnie. Hello Arnie Arnie."

I wave my hand half mockingly, half warmly. Fox and Yip both nod deadpan to me, workmanlike in understated recognition. I assume that they have a new pigeon playmate on their hands. I'm guessing/hoping. One of us is thinking that. I'm thinking they're thinking. Whatever.

Fox: "Arnie, Arnie, Arnie, Arnie. Let's see. So, Arnie." Fox strokes his pointed goatee, while loading up for his next question-incursion. "Why are you here?"

Arnie: "Because, my parents thought it was a good idea, I guess."

Yip: "Hmmmm... Well, Uncle Gabby and Aunt Blabby," my parents thought it was a good idea that I come here. So I reckon that is a good enough reason. Whaddya think, Foxy?"

Fox: "I dunno."

Yip: "You're kind of a lenient sort on this matter."

Fox: "I dunno. I'm thinking there ain't no way my parents would've got me into this place without the threat of incarceration. But, I dunno. Then again, I'm not a fuckin' mute like you."

Yip: "'Tis true, Foxy."

Me: "What's this mute stuff, anyway? You guys. What the fuck is a mute?

Yip: "Mmm. Thought you'd never ask, Android. A mute. Well, let's just say that the jury is out as to whether you are one. What we know pretty much is that you are not a cretin."

Me: "Cretin. What the fuck is that?"

Fox: "Yip, why don't you field this one? Being as how you are the world's foremost authority on cretinhood."

Yip: "Be glad to, mine Foxten. Now then, Arndroid. A cretin is one who is obviously, around here, that is, not working with a full deck, horsepower-wise. Brain damage, mine young friend. Hence, you... do not appear to these lay, but very much expert eyes, to qualify for cretinhood. However, mutated, mutation, muteness is quite another story. Entirely. I believe with all my heart that you like me, unlike the Fox, are a Mute."

Fox: "Is Yip not right? You know that for a poet, Yip, you are a bad grammarian, yes you are, Mr. Yip"

Yip: "Foxy, fuck the shut up," clucking his tongue in sync with the pronunciation of the word "up."

Me: "Why isn't the Fox here...why is he not a mute? How come? What's the deal here?"

Yip: "Well, you see, Mr. A, Mr. Fox here, my finely feathered foxy friend, is not what you would call ...insane. No, no, not Mr. Fox-man. No, no Andris. My foxy friend, um, he comes to his moniker honestly. He has earned his name, as it were. He is what is known in the industry as your basic card-carrying credit card fraudulating, ummmummmm... psychopath. Yes sir, a bona fide con man. Right here in our midst."

Foxy: "Now now, Yip. You're flattering me. You're paying me too much homage."

Yip: "I beg to differ. I simply do."

Me, growing suddenly tired: "You guys are a trip."

Yip/Fox, noticing: "Well, Arnie, I guess we'll be moseying along. See you later now."

Me, saluting, in mock-official soldierness: "Right!"

They leave and resume their pacing, the big sport on the unit. I finish my cigarette and head to my room. Again, I fall asleep with my clothes on till Nurse Berra wakes me up around 11:00 p.m. to get into my sleeping outfit. I sleep until 7:00 a.m., deadfully.

CHAPTER 31

The Next Day

The next day, waking up, breakfast, my morning medications (400mg. Thorazine, 25mg. Stelazine and 150mg. of Elavil), I am informed by nurse Berra ("Kitten" was her nickname) that I might want to walk over to the gymnasium where a bunch of patients are organizing a basketball game. Knowing about my interest in sports, she's trying to be helpful in the cheerful way that she has with the patients. "Sugary sincerity" is what I call it. Very concerned. In retrospect, possibly a little smarmy, but not saccharine. At the time, I didn't mind it.

At any rate, off to the court I go, a building away from my unit, on this snowy twelve degree overcast day in central Connecticut. Inside the gym, three patients are practicing their jump shots. Two teenagers around my age and an older guy with wavy black hair with gray streaks, the spitting image of Larry Parks in the "Jolson Story." This Larry Parks guy must be about 6'3". Fairly burly, moved well, sort of affable. That is until the game starts and it's my job to guard this guy in a two on two half-court game. He immediately goes to work on me with his inside game. Using his size, his elbows, his feet stomping, whatever it takes to gain the edge on me. I work up quite a sweat. He does, too. His team wins 11-9, a close game, he and my scoring most of the points. The other two guys mostly feeding us. I'll never forget, as we shake hands after the game, the first words he speaks to me. I ask him his name.

"O'Brian's the name, priesthood's the game," he answers with a jolly chuckle.

Taken aback, shaking my head, I manage to mumble through my disbelief, "I've seen it all. The hoodlum, lunatic priest, incarnate. Too much."

O'Brian laughs. He gets off on my directness, I guess and is quick with his response, "And you?"

"I am Arnie Brucher from New Rochelle, soon to be eighteen and getting ready to graduate high school. I'm gonna be outta here soon."

"That's good, Arnie," O'Brian says in a sympathetic tone. "That's good. As for me, I've been here eight months myself since June 6, 1967. Yep, that's right, eight months since Father McGovern dropped me off. I'll never forget that day. No sir, bad day at Black Rock. Whew. Was I in bad shape. But I'm a whole lot better now."

"When you getting out?" I ask plaintively. It's my favorite question.

"Maybe soon," O'Brian offers, "as soon as I make up my mind what I want to do about the priesthood."

Curious, I ask, “Whaddya mean?”

“Well the last couple of years of my priestly career wasn’t exactly spent involved with what are usually thought of as priestly activities, Arnie. You might say I was living it up. Wine, women and song. All three actually, and you might as well throw in gambling, too while we’re at it.”

“Whoa,” I say. “That’s pretty weird stuff,” flabbergasted but intensely interested. “I didn’t know priests did that stuff.”

O’Brian, “Well, this one did.”

Me (still open mouthed): ”That’s something.”

O’Brian: “Yup, sure is. Amazed me too at first. But I kind of developed a taste for it actually. And it sort of interfered with my responsibilities at the parish.

Me: “So, what did your monsignor say about this, I mean your bishop?”

“Actually, my bishop was pretty nice about it if you want to know the truth. But he was pretty concerned.”

Me: “About you or about the Church? “

Father O’Brian: “Hey Arnie, you’re pretty sharp... you know. Actually, about both. You’re right. “

Me: “Hmmm, heavy shit.”

Father O’Brian: “Yep. My bishop! If you want to hear the story, he was actually pretty worried about me and he heard about this place through some of the bishops who had come here, so he was able to get me in and the Church is paying for all this, believe it or not.”

Me: "Damn, pretty cool trip."

O'Brian: "Yeah, anyway that's my story, what about you?"

Me: "Well, Father, it's fairly simple. Family stuff, I guess. Father shit. I guess. I dunno. Just flipped out, I guess."

O'Brian: "Mmmm, Well, welcome aboard friend. See you at morning walk, all right? It's one of the rituals we do here. Pretty much after every meal, we stroll around the grounds, smoke our cigarettes and pace it off. A whole slew of us do it. You'll see. Come join us. Okay?"

Me: "Sure. Thanks for the offer, Father."

O'Brian: "Sure man. You'll see. It's okay here. You'll adjust."

Me: "Yeah."

O'Brian: "Anyways, Arnie, gotta go, see you around campus."

Me: "Yeah, catch you after lunch, right?"

Father: "Right."

Later the next day, I notice O'Brian reaching into his pocket, pulling out his eighteenth cigarette of the day. It's only 11:00 a.m. He would have sixty more before the day ends. I am no slouch myself, but not in O'Brian's league. When it comes to smoking, thirty to thirty-five a day is my vicinity.

Viceroys are my brand, sometimes Raleighs, occasionally Marlboros. The cigarette trip. Here, it's intense. I mean, they should have a lung specialist stationed on every unit, given the amount of cigarettes consumed. It's a way to survive the boredom, anxiety, depression, and confusion which is endemic in this place. One of the ways we mark time. You name it, we're going through it.

Anyway, I head back to my unit, Butler I, and O'Brian to his unit, Fuller II, the other unlocked unit. I immediately go to my room but am intercepted by Nurse Berra who cuts me off in mid stride to inform me that Dr. Sanding will be meeting me in 15 minutes for my first appointment. He would be my psychiatrist. Immediately, I feel a wave of anxiety. Don't ask me why. I still don't know why to this day it still happens to me thirty percent of the time before shrink appointments. Clearly, on this day I am afraid. They have the power. That must be it. And scrutinize you they will. Yeah, that's it. I dunno. I light up a Viceroy to quell my anxiety, and then another one, and then a third, then off to the doctor's building where dozens of psychiatrists and residents see their patients for individual therapy.

My shrink is a young strawberry blonde cherub who greets me in the waiting room in a soft voice. I must say, to me it feels put on. It doesn't help me feel any calmer. But maybe nothing would have helped. So, as I walk into his office, he does that usual shrink thing. He waits. I do, too. Finally, he says, "Is there something you'd like to talk about?"

I feel petrified, tongue-tied, desperately uncomfortable, really uptight. I don't know how to begin. Feeling on guard, bad, actually, feeling for the first time the reason I am here – to get better, to recover from my breakdown. That's what I feel is so real, so palpable in the doctor's office. That's what I can't 't talk about or even know that that is what I am feeling really. Just excruciating discomfort.

I begin haltingly. "I don't really know what to say, or why I'm here," I say in a barely audible voice. "Guess I had a nervous breakdown. I don't know." I avoid eye contact. The doctor is quite caring, looking concerned and compassionate. Oy. That compassionate look. It gives me the creeps and makes me feel even more fragile than I feel already. Like, "Oy, am I that fucked up?"

The doctor continues to talk in that soft voice about there being no hurry. No need for me to feel any particular way, to feel this or that, no pressure, no hurry, etc. Trying hard, working hard, no doubt. Excruciating stuff, I can tell you. It rolls off him like goo. My father, of course, comes up, girlfriends, school all that stuff. It probably was the slowest therapy hour ever, before or since, and I've had hundreds of sessions since. Finally, mercifully, it ends.

When it does, as soon as I opened Sanding's office door, I run back to my unit at a sprinter's pace, to the warmth of my bed, landing belly-flop bouncing, and simultaneously sticking the pillow over my head. I fall asleep through lunch and don't wake until 2:00 p.m. when Nurse Berra gently but persistently nudges me awake to inform me that since I slept through lunch, I could get food at the social lounge area that is open. Everything is voluntary here for me on this unit. If I choose to, I can lounge around all day. No pressure.

I head to the social area, where I immediately notice the snack bar on my right where the same group of people I saw the other day are sitting. They are five guys and two girls. Chuckling and smoking away and making snide comments to each other. Foxy is there, too. He catches my gaze, waves me over and invites me to sit down. Shyly and reluctantly, I head his way, to the group where Foxy announces,

"Everybody, I want you to meet Arnie, the mutate, who just came in from New Rochelle, living in Butler I. Arnie, say hello."

Me: "Howdy."

Fox: "Why don't you pull up a chair and have a seat?"

And I do, compliantly, next to a dark-haired slender Bogart smoking guy who looks to be in his early 20's. He immediately extends his hand and says, "I'm Mandy Milstein. Welcome aboard. We're in the middle of Pass the Ash. Care to play?"

I wasn't sure how to play, and said so. Milstein explains the rules. It's a type of truth or dare, where each person takes a drag of a cigarette and then passes it on. The person smoking when the ash falls has to answer all questions posed to them by the others. The questions are as personal and embarrassing as could be. You're expected to answer honestly. A blonde guy named Brian Boxman starts lighting up a Tareyton. Taking a deep drag and passing it to Amanda, a brunette with owl-shaped eyes, who in mock concern, quickly passes the cigarette to a guy named "Bad Trips." He's a long-haired heavy set type who inhales the cigarette like it is a marijuana joint, deeply and noisily. Unscathed, he passes it to Fox. Long now, the ash is high and tilting. Foxy spills the ash upon taking ownership. So Fox is "It."

Mandy Milstein opens the questioning with a rapid-fire delivery. "OK, Foxy, how many credit cards were on you when the Connecticut State Troopers busted you? The truth, Foxy."

Foxy: "Ummm, let's see now." He's looking like he's bothered by the question. "Seventy-five." At the response, Brian, the starter, follows up with, "What were the terms of your sentence, Mr. Fox?"

Fox: "Five years in jail or one year in the nuthouse. "

Brian: "Which did you take?"

Fox: "Umm. Umm."

Brian: "Come on Foxy, stop fucking around. The truth."

Fox: "Okay, five years in jail."

Amanda: "How many times a day do you masturbate?"

Fox: "Um, um..."

Brian: "You're fucking around again."

Fox: "Okay. Three."

Mandy Milstein, chiming in: "We have proof on film, if you will, that it is actually five times. Therefore, you are disqualified."

In watching this, I am doubly relieved. First off, that I'm not the one to drop the ash, and second, that the game isn't serious or vicious. Mandy Milstein, turning to me, suddenly begins his interrogation.

"Where are you from? What are you doing here?" Etc. Etc. "What kind of music, movies do you like?"

We discover a mutual love for the Beatles, Bogart and 30's black and white movies. Mandy Milstein expresses affection, bordering on fanaticism, for Fred Astaire and Ginger Rogers movies, which I don't share. But clearly the two of us are clicking along here. Then with no adieu, he heads to the piano and goes into what I would later find out is his trademark, leadoff song, George Gershwin's "Someone to Watch Over Me." His playing, competent and feelingful, stops the group in its tracks and most of the room as well. Melancholic, mournful and longing, his playing captures some of what I and a lot of other people in that hall are feeling. We applaud as the last notes die out. He follows that with the up-tempo "'Ain't Misbehavin'," clearly intending to trample on any maudlin sentimentality that might be lingering. It works. He goes on to play over a half dozen more standards before returning to the group.

Such flair, finesse, romantic ardor. That seals it for me. Mandy and I would be tight from then on in. After that performance, for the first time, I feel a sense of comfort and at-homeness that I hadn't felt in a while, maybe ever. The beginnings of some communal bond, I guess. I decide this place would be bearable and walk back to the unit with Fox, another elder statesman/role model for me in the ways of mental hospital survival.

CHAPTER 32

Settling In

S So I settle in. Go to class in the morning to finish school so I can graduate on time. Hang out with Mandy Milstein, Father O'Brian and the Fuller II crowd, seeing the shrink three times a week and try to tolerate the boredom, depression, homesickness and loneliness that settle in and at times, is unbearable. At first, they forbid family visits the first two or three weeks or so. So I have to wait until the beginning of March to see my parents.

The first visitors are Mom, Dad and Marla Mascowitz, who proves to be a loyal and faithful phoner and letter writer. They drive up on a Sunday, two hours up the Connecticut Turnpike to visit me.

The Sunday about three weeks before my eighteenth birthday they show and it is a fabulous reunion – for about two minutes. That is, until I see them reacting to how different I am. Drugged up, depressed, shy, somewhat timid, frightened, it isn't hard to see how disheartened they look even though they try to cover it up. Particularly, Marla, the sweet thing. She seems so disappointed, almost hurt, yet loving, but in her way a real trooper. No way she is going to let on. But, no matter. I can easily see through my parents' cheerful façade, and in a way am not surprised. It's what parents do, I think. But the pretending, the putting on of a happy face by Marla cut deeper. It feels so awkward. Them with me. Me with them.

We make small talk for two hours, if you can call it small talk. I can barely string more than a sentence together at a time. We go downtown for Chinese food and then part soon after. I don't remember ever feeling so uncomfortable. It was like I didn't belong to them anymore. In fact, I didn't.

Upon returning to the IOL, I breathe a sigh of relief and ban thoughts of Marla, Mom and Dad's reactions to me. Glad to be "home." This was where I live now. This was where I belong. Among the mutes. After all, that's what I am. Let's face it. The shrink tries to be helpful with this the next day, tries to normalize it, or be sympathetic, or whatever the fuck they do. But he can't take away the pain. They never can. No one can. He can't. It's just one big mess. No one understood. Just the guys, Mandy, Fox, Father and the gang, I guess. The gulf between me, my family, shrinks, helpers, even Marla... the gulf just seems to widen.

I sink into a deep Thorazine and Stelazine aided depression. The experience of not being able to handle the outside world is too much. I despair, cry a lot, and withdraw into myself and into the world of my patient, mutate friends. Even though I try to put a mental fence around the visit, their faces haunt me and I am overcome with pain. What follows from Mom, Dad and Marla's experience of their visit is what I pieced together later.

My parents' ride home from Hartford with Marla had all the qualities of a wake but without the drinking. My parents, of course, are beside themselves. My father and Marla, by far the most emotional, take turns breaking into spontaneous paroxysms of crying jags. Seeming to feed off each other's teariness and hurt, they are like chain reactions. Each is feeling pain and sadness for different private reasons.

Dad, obviously feeling some guilt. Marla, feeling loss and disappointment about the state of her first love, not to mention the fact that they are both concerned about me. Meanwhile, my mother is reduced to an oppressive discomfort and silence, feeling as bad but not able to release or express her sadness with tears.

Conversation, when it comes at all, becomes a mutual bucking up session. Everyone in their own way trying to accentuate the positive in the visit.

Finally falling back on such well-worn clichés as, "He's young. He'll bounce back."

"People recover from these things."

"This place is the best there is; they've helped people with Arnie's problem before."

This last phrase was one my father uses repeatedly with me on the phone and with the family. Clearly, he is putting his energies into his faith in medicine and the powers of medical psychiatry, such as it is. It is a long ride home. My mother had more fish to fry as well. She had her next oldest sister to worry about, who at the time is suffering with an advanced state of colon cancer. Mom is in a heavy place, across the board.

I feel bad for my parents and Marla especially, but quite frankly far worse for myself. I find myself devoting large amounts of time, mostly alone, trying to figure out what happened to me and why. It doesn't make sense. Hours of time are spent in my room listening to my favorite albums, mostly ballads or sad songs by the Beatles, Simon and Garfunkel, Dionne Warwick and homesick because of their evocative value. The music conjures up memories, feelings and images from my past, especially conducive for crying. I cry a lot, especially early on. There is a lot of feeling sorry for myself and my plight, a lot of, "Why me?" The routine and voluntary nature of the daily schedule leaves a lot of room for rumination, contemplation of one's navel and sorting out of one's life. Probably, some of all three.

At any rate, I indulge in rumination, finding the art therapy, leather and metal shops boring and useless and so have lots of free time in the afternoon after my morning classes. There is only so much afternoon hanging out that I can do with my mates either strolling on the campus or shooting the shit in the Lounge. I begin to take two-hour naps in the afternoon with the stereo on. The routine is pretty deadly. Deadening and predictable. My depression deepens and hardens. I am no longer that homesick now after that first visit. Faith in my capacities to get better weakened subtly and manifest in an ongoing sense of feeling shitty, coupled with a less confident experience when engaging with the outside world. My underlying worries and pessimism are largely underground until one night a month later in early April, the night of the weekly dance at the social lounge.

CHAPTER 33

We Gotta Get Outta This Place

Like most of the patients, whether on the locked or unlocked units, I am heavily medicated. This was the custom at the time, and it still is. Some of the medication is effective in reducing psychotic symptoms. Some is overkill. It dulls, zombieizes or mutes emotions. Hence the term, "mute," or I should say, one of the reasons for the "mute" moniker. As a mute, I was a mutate, short for mutant or mutation, the genetic term for a deviant cell. It should be known that psychotic people in the United States and most of Western Europe were being treated with phenothiazines – Thorazine, Stelazine, Mellaril – that had many serious side effects. I say this only to say that I was not immune to these side effects.

This one night, a couple of weeks after Marla and my parents visit, it's the weekly dance. But not the usual band catering to the Bing Crosby/Frank Sinatra set of patients, people in their 40's, 50's and 60's. Tonight, they find a band that also covers the Elvis/Beatles people, so both ends of the age spread are considered.

Before tonight, rock is confined to the units or patients' rooms. But tonight there are electric guitars, not just brass and woodwinds. Hey, but you know what? The band sucks. Their idea of rock 'n' roll sounds like Bar Mitzvah music. My friends and I are disgusted and disgruntled. Fox, Yip, Amanda, Mandy, Boxman, even Father O'Brian are, to a person, puked-out by the insipidness of the band.

Bored to the gills, I stupidly announce the fact that I like to sing. The next thing I know I'm being egged on. Mandy, Foxy and Brian Boxman are prodding the shit out of me to get on stage. I demure. I'm feeling waves of stage fright. There's no way I want to get on that stage alone.

Mandy says, "Don't worry, we'll go up there with you, singing back up. We'll be like the Pips to your Gladys, you fucking mute." And we do it.

Mandy approaches the bandleader, who quickly nods and waves us up on the stage. I know exactly what song I want to sing. One, which I later find out, has a little resonance with the Viet Nam soldier crowd. Who'd a thunk? I thought the hippies and hip people had a monopoly on that song. I am wrong. So, with the security of having Mandy, Foxy and Brian Boxman as my back up, I now give you the vocal stylings of Arnie Brucher and his fabulous backup singers, the Pukes. Let's give a fine, fine hand for Arnie and the Pukes.

In this dirty old part of the city
Where the sun refuse to shine
People tell me there ain't no use in trying,

My little girl you're so young and pretty
And one thing I know is true
You're gonna be dead before your time is due.

See my daddy in bed dying
Watched his hair been turning gray
I know he's been working and slaving
his life away, yes I know.

He's been
Working and slaving, slaving and working
Working, yeah, work, yeah, yeah, yeah, yeah

We gotta get out of this place
If it's the last thing we ever do
We gotta get out of this place
Girl, there's a better life for me and you.

That famous Animals ditty of a few years ago. Up until now I didn't know that that song was appropriate to me. I acquiesce partially realizing and partially not realizing the massive impact that singing the song might have on me. Well, I sing it, with Mandy, Foxy and

Boxman doing backup. They are out of tune with me, but our harmonies make up for it. And we all sing with gusto and genuine enthusiasm.

In the middle of the song, I feel waves of anxiety beginning to surge. But it is not until the song ends that the force of it really hits me. Increasingly uncomfortable, I have to keep moving – fast, first, inside the dance hall and then soon after, outside to get air. But no relief. Finally, I talk to an aid as the panic begins to escalate. The aid, an older gentleman, gently walks me outside, back to my unit, where I begin to pace, agitated, intensely, more and more. Unable to calm myself, pulse racing, palms sweating, thoughts of losing control of my body beginning to invade my consciousness. Fears of imminent loss of bodily control dominating my mind, obsessively, rapidly. No relief. No help. Fear. Scared I will die. Start to gasp for air. Nurse Berra, seeing my discomfort, suggests that I get a shot, an intramuscular shot of Thorazine. I decline thinking I can overcome this state on my own without the shot. What follows is thirty minutes of more pacing, gasping for air, fear of losing control, and pervasive thoughts that my body will force me to commit a self-destructive act that I really do not want to commit.

The more I try to put these thoughts out of my mind, the stronger they get. Finally, the anxiety is way too overwhelming. I am wound up like a clock, spinning with the stuff. I approach Nurse Berra, desperately and resignedly, with my assent for the shot. It hurt. The needle penetrated my tuchus tissue. I try not to flinch. But, no doubt I do with the pain and horror of the needle penetrating my skin. Miraculously, the sedating effects of the drug comes on in twenty minutes. Drowsiness follows, followed by conking out and a ten hour sleep, dead to the world.

This episode is the beginning of a six weeklong daily binge of panic/anxiety attacks, eventuating in almost daily intramuscular Thorazine shots. Then, suddenly and inexplicably, the anxiety subsides. I still don't know why. During this period, one of the worst follow-up panic attack episodes occurs in class.

We're reading the book *Man Alone,* a book on the myriad forms of alienation, in my Problems of American Democracy class. Sitting in class with my fellow high school mutates, now two weeks into the anxiety attacks, the content of the articles, alienation from work, alienation from others, alienation from oneself... are getting to me. They're talking about me. They're definitely talking about me. Fuck. A combo plate of, I suck, sinking into the lowlands, fighting against it – and you got your basic anxiety state. Fight, fight, fight. The more I fight, the worse it gets. Yet I can't not fight. I hate how this feeling feels. Hate feeling scared. Push it away. Push it away. Anxiety escalates. Gotta leave the class. Don't say anything to the teacher. Just bolt. Gone. Back to the unit for my Thorazine shot. Hate this. Hate this. Hate this life. Hate my life. Fuck.

But then it's over. Only six weeks of this shit. But somehow it ends. Marla, my parents, Mark, Rick and some female friends show up during this period. It's my lowest. I'm almost mute, extremely uncomfortable around people in the outside world. I'm in the "Velt Arien," the world outside the ghetto. Can't get my thoughts together.

Avoid eye contact as much as I can. Ashamed, embarrassed. Inward. Hate looking at the sad or alarmed looks of my friends, parents, Marla. Fuckarama. Six weeks of hell.

CHAPTER 34

Data Processing

That's who we're playing, "Data Processing." I don't even know what data is. Some fancy recordkeeping system. Who knows? These data processing guys, guys in their 20's and 30's, nice guys, regular guys, they negotiate with Mandy Milstein to play us every Tuesday night after dinner. They're decent players. Probably a little out of shape. But we, for some reason, are a talented lot of cuckoo birds.

Mandy Milstein is at short, good range, a doubles and singles man, our leadoff hitter. Brian Boxman hits to all fields, decent power, plays third, bats second. By far our best player, ability-wise, is Father O'Brian. He's our first baseman, tremendous power, dead arm, no wind. Four packs of Larks a day takes care of that. Freeman, my roommate, he's the cleanup hitter. Either hits a homerun or pops up. When he hits a homer, he whoops it up like he's Babe Ruth or something. When he pops up, he throws his bat, talks to himself out loud in the third person for five minutes with negative nasty epithets. Me, I'm in left field, batting fifth. Good fielder, erratic hitter, surprising power, very fast, average arm. Lem, the new guy, is our pitcher. We play modified fast pitch, no windmill wind up. Throw as fast as you can.

Oh, yeah. We're ready. Bored stiff and loaded for bear. In honor of the festivities, Mandy has some tee shirts stenciled for the team. Each T-shirt is fitted with a number and nickname/diagnostic category on the back. Mine was "Senile Psychosis," Mandy's was "Sick Fuck," Boxman's "Soap Opera Dependency Syndrome." O'Brian's was the longest: "Blasphemy, Heresy. Prognosis: Hell and/ or Limbo. Definitely Purgatory" – or something like that. It takes a little time to read the T-shirts.

Data Processing finds it amusing, but they don't laugh when Milstein opens the top of the first with a double, followed by a Boxman single down the left field line, followed by O'Brian's future COPD riddled, breathless, inside-the-park homerun. Then Freeman Taylor's solo blast, or "tater", as he was fond of calling it. Instantly it was 4-0. The game was no contest really. Outfielding, outhitting, and outrunning them, we romp to an easy 13–4 win.

That was the first of twenty such games that we played through mid-September. In all, we win nineteen of them. So, I guess we're good at something. The World Series Champs of Mental Institutional Softball, whoopee. The first night's win is good for a sixteen-hour-long good mood, my longest in three months, if you don't count the manic episode back in January as a good mood. And I don't. That win gives us Mutes, conversational material for days. Yesiree, Bob.

But before I get carried away, softball games in general and this victory specifically, is the lone highlight in an otherwise monotonous pace of numbing sameness. My parents visit me now every three weeks. This is basically torture all around. Long silences, phony small talk, desperate optimism, straightjacketed nods and grimaces on my side, parents walking on eggshells. Me, the eggshell.

I get weekly or biweekly phone calls from Marla. By this time, I don't have much to say to her either. Marla, her usual bubbly self, fills me in on social goings on, breakups, going steadies, drug busts, racetrack highlights. Marla is a real plugger, trying to keep the energy up, doing her best.

One night late in May, she tells me she is asked to what would be my Senior Prom, but wants to check with me first. I tell her to go ahead. The thought of my being allowed to go to my Senior Prom is unthinkable. My heart sinks, but I can't imagine I will be given a pass home for that. I seem too fucked up. I am wrong. The next day, prissy, sincere, sensitive Dr. Sanding "explores" the issue with me. He says, "Why not?" I can't believe it. I know I want to and try not to think about what it might really be like.

Drugged up on Thorazine and other drugs, the deal is struck: a three day pass and an option to go to graduation. I am actually eligible, having diligently gone to classes the past four months and getting passing grades with half the effort and one tenth the energy and concentration that I am used to. I am eligible for the diploma.

The trip home is inaugurated by a family therapy session with my parents and two brothers, my psychiatrist and a chain smoking, nervous social worker. The session focuses on me as the "Identified Patient ," a family systems term for my role as patient which I guess the therapists try to move me away from by sharing the wealth, or blame as it were. What I don't like about my father, blah, blah, blah, how he is, who he is, how he should be more sensitive to my feelings, or how I should be more thick-skinned. Brothers Dave and Lew are mostly left out of it. Mom functions as an observer mostly. It's mostly Dad vs. me, or me vs. Dad. Usual bullshit. We leave Hartford right after the session. I am excited, filled with anticipation but numb and sedated.

The trip home has its moments. My dad's apparently in a good mood. His son is coming home. In the middle of the ride, somehow, he gets onto one of his World War II stories which are always a source of amusement, except usually we've heard them thirty times already. This is a new one. Maybe it has to do with the unusual circumstance of my coming home. Maybe that triggers the memory. Can't really say. This is the scene.

Dad's the driver. Dave, Lew, and me in back in the middle, sitting in our birth order as usual, and mom in front. Dad going about fifty-five down the New England Thruway. Dad begins.

Dad: "So, I'm in North Africa, see. It's 1943. We'd just driven Rommel into retreat. And the English are there too, you understand. You know, Montgomery's guys. Old Blood and Guts, Patton is leading us, that son of a bitch. We're out on the desert, the 7th Division, and I see this English artillery guy walking away from his tank, all sweaty and everything. He's all red faced and kicking the sand in front of him about ten feet from the tank he's been driving. The tank is looking a little lopsided. "

"So I walk up to him, getting out of the Jeep I'm riding in. And first, I salute, which is the protocol. He's a major and I'm only a lieutenant at the point. And then I says, 'Hey, Major. What's the matter? Is anything wrong?'"

"Well, the Major he looks up to me and says in his best King's English, 'You bet there is, mate.'"

"So I says back to him, 'Yeah, what is it?'"

"So he says back to me, 'Well, if you really want to know,' pointing to the tank."

"And I say, 'Yeah, if you want to tell me, Major.'"

"All right, mate," the English guy says. "You see that thing over there?"

"I says, 'Yeah. I see it.'"

"The English guy finally, 'Well, that thing. That bloody thing. Well. The Fucking Fucker is Fucked!'"

Dad can barely get the words out in his best English before he erupts into his machine gun laugh that's always completely contagious. The next thing we know, we're all erupting in explosions of yaks, guffaws, knee-slapping, chest-thumping tear-inducing paroxysms of riotous laughter. So out of control is the hilarity and coughing that Dad has to pull off the road to avoid an accident. Machine gun hilarity. It proves to be the last smile of the next three days. The rest is a rearguard, shields-up performance.

The world is clearly a dangerous place psychologically, maybe physically. At that level of consciousness, there's no ability to distinguish between the two. I'm experiencing the physical and the psychological as one thing. I'm fragile, vulnerable with self-esteem in the minus column. Bogey facade not available.

My pals, Marla, teachers, are all thrilled to see me. Extremely nice, very uncomfortable. The world feigning normality around me, I can see them trying. I'm trying, too. It's bad.

Then, there's the Senior Prom itself. Wearing a black tuxedo, in mid-June, ninety degrees, ninety percent humidity, everyone's in white or light blue. I guess I'm sticking out like a sore thumb. And I feel and probably look like cardboard in that tux.

Dionne Warwick, herself, is the entertainment. People seem happy, excited, drunken, and stoned. I'm thinking, what the fuck am I doing here? Going through the motions like I belong. It's a joke. I'm not even here with Marla. I'm here with one of her friends, Lorna. Marla's here, but she's with somebody else, because I didn't think I could go. So she accepted an invite from another guy, a guy who I know a little. He's okay, as far as I'm concerned. I don't really care.

Lorna is sweet. She drops me off home at eleven. I bolt to my room, avoiding my parents, take off my clothes in seconds, lights out, completely relieved to be home in my bed. The next Sunday, my parents drive me back to Hartford with the usual pep talks, silence, and small talk. I am glad to be home, my *real* home – the IOL. Yes fans, I have been thoroughly INSTITUTIONALIZED at the INSTITUTE OF LIVING.

CHAPTER 35

The Fire and The Hole

July 4th weekend. Back at Butler I after the abortive home visit for my Senior Prom. Cozy cocoon. This IOL, safe from the cares of the world-weary, battle-torn country. In the four and a half months since I've been here at the IOL, we've already seen Martin Luther King killed in Memphis and riots in the streets in numerous major cities. LBJ is making clear he will not run for reelection, that he will neither seek nor accept the nomination of his party. And riots at Columbia University, riots at the Sorbonne, nearly leading to a revolution in Paris. Bobby Kennedy is killed in L.A. on the night of the California primaries. Bobby Kennedy, who was the presumptive nominee and then probably would have been the next president of the United States. For me, it's Thorazine burgers. Endless bloodlust, revenge, hate and strife for the U.S. I wish I could participate. I get a taste of it nine months earlier during the March on the Pentagon and am now sufficiently radical-liberalized and have significant questions about the efficacy of electoral politics.

Tales of the SDS and the Black Panther Party start to drizzle in as residue from the Columbia uprising and Northern California, Oakland, Berkeley where the Black Panther Party is planting its flag. I am, besides feeling sorry for myself, angry and resentful that I can't be out there protesting with the rest of my generation. All I can think of are ways to amuse myself. Comic voices resound in my head. I start to announce my life as a way to pass the time. In the past, when I announced my life, sportscasters like Mel Allen, Red Barber or the new Knick announcer, Marv Albert, made their appearance. Sometimes I did the impressions to people who could relate to sports. Other times, I kept the impressions to myself, chuckling quietly.

Anything to alleviate the fucking boredom. My newest impression comes not from the world of sports broadcasting but from the world of stand up comedy. A strange choice, in that I hate this man's politics and don't really think he's that funny. But he's such a ubiquitous presence on TV that it's impossible to not notice him. Of course, I am talking about the grandmaster of ceremonies of most Oscars, that guy who teamed up with Bing Crosby to do nine road pictures. Come on out here and give a big round of applause, for you know, the one, the only... Mr. Bob Hope.

"Thank you. I gotta tell you. It's great to be back in Hartford, Connecticut. Back here at, you know, the Institute of Living. You know my old pal, that great improv stand up, you know the great Johnny Winters. Yeah, that's right. You know he used to live here. Yup, you know where your boy Mandy and Father O'Brian live, well back in 60. Yeah that's right. Old Johnny, well, he got a little whacky after an appearance at the Hungry I, or was it the Purple Onion, I'm not sure."

"Anyway, old Johnny, well he got this cuckoo idea that he'd go down into old Fisherman's Wharf in San Francisco. Yup, old Johnny, well, he thought he'd just climb one of those old yachts down there. Yes, he did. And you know what he did. Sure as you're born, he climbed up one of the mastheads. I do not tell a lie. And he was swinging from the masthead, maybe thirty feet high. Yeah, old Johnny he was swingin', hootin' and hollerin', until the people at Alioto's Restaurant, well they got wind of it and, too bad for ole Johnny Winters, they called the fuzz on him. And yup, you know what? First, they took him to the hoosegow. But the fuzz didn't really know what to do with him. So, yup. You guessed it, they shipped him all the way here. Yup, the IOL, so it's great to be back where ole Johnny Winters is one of our great alumni. Let's give a hand for Johnny Winters. All right!"

Yeah, all of that's true, Bob. Johnny was an alumnus of Fuller II, back in 1960. Kind of gave the place some cache. But, I'm straying here. I'm trying to tell you about life back at the IOL following my abortive Senior Prom and how deadingly dull and boring it is, yet safe, to be back.

Chemically straightjacketed, but my body starting to get used to the effects of Thorazine, Stelazine and Elavil, and now the anticholinergic, Cogentin, too that manages the extrapyramidal symptoms that makes my body fold up like a pretzel if I don't have this drug. I'm starting to build up a tolerance to these drugs. I kind of, in a strange way, find a halfway point between the old Arnie and the new Arnie. A fifty per cent mark of personality, if you will. Thorazinized, but getting used to it. Stelazinized, but getting used to it. Elavilized, but getting used to it. Cogentinized, but getting used to it. In in-between land. Less dry mouth, less stuporification, less lethargy, less torpor. A little more energy. A little. Still, I'm an internal political prisoner. I haven't been arrested for any political or criminal acts, for that matter nor have I done anything that immoral or unethical.

My only sin is in failing to master my physical and social environment adequately. I can't live with my parents. I can't live at home in New Rochelle. I lack the "ego strength," according to my shrink. Some might say, post Thorazine, that I lack an ego. Mine, at any rate is in shards. Shattered. I am dependent. Dependent on the kindness of strangers, as Blanche DuBois once so perfectly and pathetically put it in "A Streetcar Named Desire." I'm relying on the "kindness of strangers." Yup, these IOL staffers sure are nice. Oh yeah. No shock treatments for this reporter. No man. No psychosurgery for me. No lobotomy for this man. No insulin shock therapy. Nope. No, just good old-fashioned, relatively noninvasive western medicine, pharmacology. Good old allopathic, symptom reduction western medicine.

Medication for my disturbed chemically imbalanced, dopamine depleted brain. Yes, and psychoanalytic psychotherapy for my deranged, distorted, out-of-touch mind.

We have school classes, if you like. We have rec time, if you like. We have everything you need here, Mrs. Robinson. Make yourself at home. Enjoy your stay. No locked units for you. We understand, Arnie. WE *really* do. Yes, we're here for you. OH, yes we are. We care about you, Arnie. WE *truly* do. We want you to get well. We do. We do. Oh yes, we do, we do, we doobee do. YOU'll get better. You're already improving. We can see. Just you wait. Have faith, Arnie. Your doctor says you're doing fine, Arnie. Yes he does, Arnie. We're sorry, that your trip home didn't go better. We're truly sorry, Arnie. Maybe next time, okay. In the meantime, there's leather, there's occupational therapy, there's woodshop, there's ceramics and there's social hour. There's volleyball and ping pong and a lot of dandy games. What ain't we got... We ain't got dames. Oh yes, oh yes.

I feel so loved and cared for that I don't know what to do. Actually, I can't think or feel anything really. It really doesn't matter. Chemically induced depression, environmentally supported by a caring institutional and parental response. My ego and self-esteem... never felt better. I swear to God. NOT.

So, anyways, I keep getting off the point. You know psychotos will do that. We get terribly loose or tangential or circumstantial, take your pick. But I'm gonna try to stick to the story here. So, anyways, one Monday morning in early July, a couple of weeks after my first visit home, Yip and I are chewing the fat in the hallway next to the nurses' station. We're smoking Marlboro after Marlboro. It's about 10:30 a.m. and we're the only ones on the unit, except of course for "Kitten" Nurse Berra, that smarmy bitch but she's busy doing her charting: meds and behavioral analysis of patients. You know, the usual "useful" stuff.

Yip and I are bored. We're bullshitting about the Black Panthers, Eldridge Cleaver, Black Power and radical politics, Yip's specialty. After all, his name was Yip after YPSL, Young People's Socialist League. The death of the Democratic Party. He loves to talk about that shit. YIP is an aficionado of radical politics, particularly Black Power politics. Rumor has it, which Yip won't confirm, that Yip's parents, Uncle Gabby and Aunt Crabby, put him in the IOL because of his refusal to date white women. Yip would neither confirm nor deny the reason for his hospitalization, but is proud of the fact that he is committed to dating only Black women. So, we're fooling around with the ashcan, absentmindedly, I might mention. You know, throwing papers in there, in crumpled form, smoking, and occasionally throwing a match or two in the can, just ta, you know, kind of see what would happen, I dunno, seeing the bright light that the fire makes in the can. It's kinda interesting. I dunno. Not really paying attention, just kind of relaxing. See, we're mental patients, so we don't have much judgment, or concentration, for that matter. Can't think too well. Not too good. Don't go blaming us now 'cause, um, we're just passing the time.

But wouldn't you know it, here comes Nurse Berra, the Kitten. She smells smoke coming out of the trash can. She's darting over to the can, red-faced and hopping mad, but she speaks in her patented concerned voice after putting the fire out herself with her shoe. The fire was about two inches high. Smoke was a low billow.

Kitten speaks, "I'm gonna have to tell your doctors about this. We cannot have this kind of behavior. It's dangerous. Not safe. You two should be ashamed of yourselves. You're in trouble. Please go to your rooms until your doctors call over for you. I'll let you know. In the meantime, you're both confined to your rooms. Now go. Go, go, go."

Soon, Dr. Sanding is at the door to my room. "Arnold. I'm so disappointed to hear of this incident. What was upsetting you? Was it your visit? Was it something about being here? Was it your girlfriend? Arnold, please, talk to us. But you must know that we can't have you and your friend starting fires. You will both have to go to North I – indefinitely."

Me: "Wow...."

North I------ the PIT, The HOLE. North I, where the cretin lifers go: Duke the Puke, Frank the King, Bernie the Puffer, and the infamous Fisherman. Oh God, oh shit. Sent down to the locked unit. North I. 1:1 constant supervision. No privileges. Deep 6, city man. Bring your cigarettes. You're gonna need them, man. You are in deep shit now. People were known to spend months down there. It's rugged. Some crazy motherfuckers there. They ain't never getting out.

"Be careful," Yip tells me. He's going to North II. Another hole for felons, the criminally insane, actively psychotic, actively suicidal characters. North I has more chronic cretins. North II, more acute cretins. Both places harboring dangerous characters. Violent, unpredictable, impulsives, compulsives.

"Watch your ass, literally and figuratively," Yip tells me. He's a veteran of these places. Been down there a couple of times before I entered the IOL.

I'm actually a bit nervous. I get my first bona fide adrenaline rush in four months, breaking through the

Thorazine stupor and numbnatude. Something tells me I better be alive for this event. On my toes, hyper vigilant, I believe you'd say.

"I will stay alert," I say to Yip. We wish each other luck.

North I--- The Hole. Lifer time down here. Better mind your P's and Q's, sir. You are with some irrational folks now. Violent, crazy motherfuckers. Better keep your distance. You ain't got your buds with you, matey. You be on your own, you dig? No Yip or Fox to show you the ropes down here, to fill you in. No Mandy Milstein or Father O'Brian to shoot the shit with about Bogart movies or Fred and Ginger movies. No Freeman Taylor to share your room with here and talk about hittin' "taters." No. There'll be no more listening to Uncle Bob's new album, "John Wesley Harding," like you did with Freeman down here. You in trouble, boy. You won't even have Brian Boxman around to bullshit with about the old Brooklyn Dodgers or the Donna Reed show, which incidentally was the correct answer to what show was Brian watching when the cops came and hauled him away to the nuthouse, following his first suicide attempt. No Andris, as Yip referred to me frequently. There wouldn't be any of these kind of guys, or girls, for that matter. No mutates at all. Nope. No mutes. Just watch your ass. They got murderers here, shell-shocked WWII guys. We got your catatonic, your paranoid and your simple schizophrenics as well as everyone's favorite, the hebephrenic. We got your organic cretins, your sexual psychotic psychopaths, now too old and burnt out. We got your child molesters galore. No women down here. They got their own lockup unit. We got a lot of staff. I'm primed.

Tuesday morning. I go down to North I after meeting with the shrink. Sanding, who is "so disappointed" and "upset" to hear that I started that fire – the little fairy. Fuck him. North I for at least a week, maybe two. It all depends on you... Luke. I can be a nice guy or I can be one son of a bitch. It all depends on you, Luke, I'm thinking. "What we got here is a failure to communicate" from one of my favorite scenes from "Cool Hand Luke" reverberating in my brain.

Fuck you, Dr. Sanding. Fuck me, I guess. I fucked up. I guess. Better get used to it. Smoke your Viceroys, Marlboros and shut up. Do your pacing, don't talk to anyone you don't know. Mind your fucking business. Listen to the radio and keep your distance. And I mean literally. Keep your fucking distance. Do not share cigarettes. This will create a firestorm. No pun intended. Just play it cool boy, real cool, like I'm a Jet in "West Side Story" before the rumble.

Where was I? Oh yeah, North I. Tuesday morning. There are twenty-five guys here. Twelve aids. One on two, fast break. Up on Butler, there was one nurse with two aids for twenty-five patients. What a ratio of staff. Fuck it. Here on North I it's crowded as shit. "Nowhere to run. Nowhere to hide," baby. Shut up Martha Reeves and the Vandellas. What am I? A walking Wurlitzer? Every fucking sentence reminds me of a song. What am I? Little Richard here. Knock it off, will you?

Fuck you, man. Tell your fucking story before your readers get bored with your flight of ideas and loose associations and put the fucking book down. Get back to it already. I'm getting sick and tired of my own goddamn loose associational antics. Pay attention. Tell 'em what happened Tuesday, when I meet the illustrious stars of North I. Go ahead. "Tell 'em. Tell 'em, tell 'em right now "(Exciters-Tell 'em 1962). Ok, I will .

You see, you don't have to be alone when you are a schizophrenic. You can talk to yourself. Play all the parts. Hallucinations, hearing voices, nah, just pure loneliness, isolation. Plain and simple. The brain gets lonely, needs company. Pussy would be good. Company, almost as. Goddamn it, tell the people about the North I all-star team already, will you. God. Yah, nah. Okay. Okay... I will. Okay. Okay. Okay. Um, um, um, um. Damn, this Thorazine makes it hard to think straight. Now I'm having pleasant associations.

Anyway, I'll try again. Here they are. The North I all-stars. I meet all of them this morning at the North I group area. So, batting first, and leading off, number 6, Bernie the Barf, alias Bernie the Puffer – two years in stirs. Catatonic. Schizophrenic. Don't talk much. Bernie's here. Watch him. They watch him all the time. A little on the compulsive side, this Bernie is. Smokes a cigarette in four seconds. Hyperventilates. Limit him to one cigarette per hour. A pleasure to watch him with that cigarette. Lights up. Eyes like pinball machines. Can't get enough draw on that puff, can you,

Bernie? I know you love that cigarette. I'm pacing and watching him. He's amazing. He paces, too. So does Duke.

Batting second and playing center field is number 4, Duke the Puke. Duke likes to chow down and barf his brains out. Don't mention that to him and don't call him "Duke the Puke" to his face Yip told me or he'll attack you physically. "Don't do it now," I can hear my maid Zee's voice in my head warning me. "Don't do it now, Arnie. Don't do it." All right already, I won't. Old Duke here's a speed merchant. Paces fast. He cuts a wide swathe. Known to flail his elbows. Watch him. I am. I do.

Meanwhile, stepping up to the podium here on North I and batting third, wearing number 3, none other than the great one. They call him the King. Ladies and gentlemen, I must tell you that the King Frank Luger has been occupying this space, if you will, these past twenty-three yars, yes indeedy, ever since the battle of Iwo Jima. Lost a few men, there, I'm told. Frank escaped that battle intact, in the material sense. Unfortunately, he forgot something. I mean to say, he left something back there in Iwo. His fucking mind. Psychological bits of his mind – shrapnel. Shrapnel, splattered every which away. Franky, you're the best. The King of North I. God love you, and may the world live in peace.

Poor Frank. Iwo Jima. Hamburger Hill. Tet Offensive. Gettysburg, Birmingham, Alabama, Berkeley, California, Chicago, Prague. For the victims, it's all the same. Aggression, gone amok. Shattered bodies, souls. Mental shrapnel. The guy is spending his time looking for bits of his shattered mind that splattered and fragmented on the beaches of Iwo Jima. The poor sick fuck. I wonder how much death he witnessed. I wonder how much death he perpetrated. Franky can smoke two cigarettes an hour. He salutes when he greets you. Dude never got out of the Army. But alas, when you get right down to it, there's really not much to say about Frank. Just another casualty of our good war WWII.

I would instead like to take this opportunity to introduce you to our cleanup hitter of North I, the Fisherman. I know, you're all wondering how did the Fisherman get his name. Dare you ask? Well don't, unless, you got the stomach for it, ladies. And, dare I say it, gents as well. So, before your run off and turn on the T.V. or some such escape, I must tell you about the Fisherman. My pal, good ole pal o' mine. The Fisherman. He's a shy kind of guy. Kind of quiet. Keeps to himself. Down here we kinda all keep to ourselves. You understand. He's a rotund kinda guy. Horn rims, doofy smile. Sad sack. Kind of pathetic. But look I gotta tell you how he got his name.

Get this. The Fisherman likes to fish. But where you ask. Ah, there's the rub. Where? Yes. Where? Well, there ain't no lakes, no rivers, nor oceans here. No reservoirs or brooks neither. Just your basic toilet bowl. And old duke, yup, Old Fish Boy, he likes to go fishing without a net or a pole, just sort of pull 'em out with his bare hands, you see. More sensual that way. More, should I say, tactile. We enjoy him. He's our friend. Our cleanup hitter. Old Fish Face. He's the Fisherman. NO net. Just gets his head and hands way down in that bowl and sure as you're born, just pulls 'em out. I hear tell, when nobody's looking, been known to take a taste, too. Kind of likes it fresh. NO cooking facilities here. So the fisherman, yeah he likes his toilet FISH, kinda raw. Yummy. He's our boy. I hope you like him and our little all-star team. A real murderers' row. Bernie, Duke, Frank and Fisherman.

So, there you have it. I'm spending a week here with the cretins. Jeez-us Christ. What the fuck am I supposed to do? Cigarettes and AM radio. Fuck you. I ain't ever gonna see the shrink. Fuck this. Where's my aid? Get me a cigarette, aid. Sir, man, you fucking scumbag, I say to myself, silently, only occasionally slightly mumbling. It's so slow here. Nothing to do. I can't read. I can't watch T.V. I can't sit. I'm a walking man. Up and back, back and over, across and over the floor's diamond shapes. There's a lot of traffic. Sometimes ten folks at a time. Five up and five back. I tune into the songs. "Reach out in the Darkness. Reach out in the Darkness. I think it's so groovy now that people are finally getting together, think it's wonderful that people are finally getting together," cowboys and girls. I remember, when we used to play shoot 'em up, bang baby. July '68. AM radio. Hartford station. "Can you surrey, can you picnic, woah , can you surry, can you picnic?" " Dance to the music, dance to the music."

Eight hours a day. Monotonous. Hit the bed. Play with pud. Now it's sleepy time down south. Fall asleep for eight hours. Get up the next day. Observe the freak show. Smoke, pace and nap. Singing, the aid, "Mr. Brucher, your doctor will see you now. I'll take you to the doctor's cottage."

Dr. Sanding: "Well, Arnold. How's it going? Learned your lesson? We think you have. We're gonna send you back to Butler I. You've handled yourself well down there."

Me: "I'm a great guy, doc."

Sanding: "Yes. Well, you can get your stuff, give it to the aid and he will bring your stuff and escort you back to Butler. But please, Arnold, no more fires!"

Me back at him in a monotone voice: "Yah, sir!!"

Walking back through the tubes, the underground tunnel, the catacombs of the hospital with their creaky spiral stairway, I'm thinking about my session with Dr. Sanding and his utter failure to comprehend anything about me other than my overt behavior and its relationship to institutional requirements. False self, phony bullshit. No help here. No way. I'm on my fucking own with this scumbag. I gotta get out of here. It's been five months now. No fucking end in sight. I'm getting worse. Goodbye North I. Those poor devils. Fuck you, Sanding. Fuck you nurses. Fuck you aids. Fuck you data processing. Fuck you Dad. Fuck you Ma. Fuck you brother Dave. Fuck you.

I'm on my own here. There is no help. Compliance is easy. That's not help. That's playing the fucking game. It speaks to about one tenth of my personality, one tenth of anything real, my feelings, thoughts, wishes, desires, beliefs, cares, concerns, needs, conflicts, problems, dilemmas, issues. Fuck. This world sucks. We're all prisoners. Inmates. Lunatics. Who's crazier? The masters or the slaves? The masters. They think they know. The slaves know they don't. The slaves just know that the fucking masters are also nuts and we won't go along. Not in our hearts. Not in our guts. Not in our souls. We play. We behave. Those stupid fucking people. Out in the world. Afraid of cops. Afraid of criminals, afraid of bosses, afraid of people with dirt on their hands. Afraid of crazies or anyone different from them. Afraid of Blacks, afraid of fags, afraid. Afraid.

I'm not afraid. Not of them and not of us. Fuck'em. I'm getting out. We're almost back to Butler I and I think, I gotta make a plan to show these fuckers that I'm sane. They fall for that crap all the time. Stupid assholes. Act nice. Be polite. Don't let on what you're thinking or feeling, needing or wanting. They're not really interested. They will lock your ass up. They will medicate your ass. They will not tolerate it. They will not tolerate any authentic, genuine expression.

So talk to your friends. Not to them. The shrinks are out. Feed them the phony bullshit. They eat that shit up. They like it. Don't talk to the aids, nurses, small talk and that's all. Confine your discussions to Mandy Milstein, Father O'Brian and Brian Boxman – and that's all. Taylor, my old roommate, is gone. Fox is gone. They're back on the streets now. You're all alone on Butler I. Your friends are gone. You're the headman. You must set an example now for your mates and plan your termination from this fucking place.

CHAPTER 36

Back on Butler

Yip is back and just in time for Lincoln Park, Yippies, cops. Mayor Daley, "The police are not here to create disorder, they are here to preserve disorder." Abbie, Jerry, Tom Hayden. SDS, Yippies. It's ugly. The Whole World is Watching. Yip and I are crying mad. Hopping. Furious. Like to kill us a pig, we say to each other in my room. For his high crimes and misdemeanors, Yip has just finished a month on North II.

His impeachment-level crime: Not progressing sufficiently. Being unreconstructed. Not willing to play ball with the powers that be.

I'm imagining the caring professionals sitting around clicking their tongues with knitted brows saying, "Quite frankly, we don't know what to do with this young man. Maybe this will teach him a lesson, and teach him the value of his relative freedom in an open unit, Butler I. Put him in stirs. Lock down. Constant supervision, then maybe he'd see how much a gift 'freedom' is." But Yip has been here for two and a half years, ladies and gentlemen. Why?

We still don't know. Uncle Gabby and Aunt Flabby, or whoever, his parents, they don't like his choice of women – Black girls, exclusively. Or his politics, for that matter. YPSL, Young People's Socialist League. Yip, Gabby and Flabby reason, needs protective custody. He needs to learn. We need to protect him against his own worst instincts. Paternalism, Fascism, Social Control. Upper Class Protective Custody.

If you're poor and don't play ball, you go to jail, or go into the military, go to Nam or get a job. Maybe.

If you're white, middle class and up, you either go to college, go to work, maybe, or go to the mental hospital. Private, not public. There's a world of difference between private mental institutions and public. The public nut houses are really like hospitals or institutions. Crowded and hyper-controlled. Forget about treatment. Medication to the max. Don't try to ask for help, because the "Cops don't need you and man they expect the same," (Bob Dylan's "Just like Tom Thumb Blues." Side two, song three "Highway 61 Revisited)."

If you're super-rich, go to Europe, go to private college, or go to a sanitarium – like the IOL, Menninger's, Chestnut Lodge, Austin Riggs.

Vee must have order. The Youth of America must learn how to *BEHAVE*. Decorum is very important. Our children must not mingle with each other, especially Black and White. They must not do drugs. Must keep a clear head to do the work of the Man. They must learn the values to be proper foot soldiers in the capitalist machinery. They must respect our property, above all (1% own 40% of all property, most, if not all, white). These are the things that we cherish. And they must be respected and adhered to. If they can't, well then they must be sent where they can learn it. We're sorry, but that is just the way it is. Nam. Jail. Nut House.

Uncle Gabby and Aunt Flabby. Upper class German Jews. Upper East Side of Manhattan. Fabulous people. Two and a half years for Yip at the IOL and bupkis has changed. Yip has not changed an iota. Not even on meds. Actually, the truth, if you wanna know, is *the man is not crazy*. A bit of a nonconformist. Yes. A great poet, though, definitely. My fucking salvation, I'm telling you.

This scene on television, with the riots in Lincoln Park and Grant Park at the Democratic convention, is really disturbing. The Pigs are clubbing *US*. They hate us. They think we're snot-nosed white kids, which we are. Don't appreciate how great this country is, which we don't. Pigs hate us. We hate them. We hate each other. Generation and class gap. Vietnam, Kennedy. Jack and Bobby – dead. King dead. Black Power. Black Panthers. "Off the pig." The Revolution has come... Time to pick up the gun. Bobby Seale, Huey Newton, Eldridge Cleaver, Kathleen Cleaver. Butler I. T.V. Out of action. Out of commission. I gotta get out of here. I gotta get out of here. I gotta get outta here.

Fellas, I'm gonna. I swear. For real. I'm gonna get real calm. See. Quiet-like. Real controlled-like. Real controlled, see. Real rational. Yeah. They like that here. Speak the King's English. Yeah. Those FUCKS. Keep my rage to myself. Yeah. No emotion. NO emoting.

No mo'. No mas. That's the plan. Gonna talk to asshole Sanding tomorrow. I want a fucking discharge date. That fucking cherubic, peach-fuzz shaped rolly polly, okie dokie, motherfucker. Scumbag. I want my date.

CHAPTER 37

Mandy Milstein's Out

So Yip and I are watching people getting beaten up on the tube. It's pretty bloody. Images of Mayor Daley blasting Abe Ribicoff inside the convention, veins bulging, bulldog snarl. An anti-Semitic vibe. You want it, we got it. Rubin, Hoffman, Hayden, Rennie Davis and Bobby Seale, the so-called "outsider agitators" busted – major ugliness. The whole world *is* watching. Feels kinda eerily safe inside these here hallowed, mutated walls. On the other hand, I wish I was there. Yip is far more rabid-avid about the whole thing. YPSL and all. Knows the players, issues, history, and party conflicts. The Democrats – McCarthy liberals, Kennedy liberals, Peace and Freedom Party, the Yippies, the Hippies, SDS, the whole shebang. Me, I just miss the action. The action of being in a crowd of like-minded people trying to do something. It's like I'm fed up. Yip, in contrast, seems so docile about getting out. I don't get it. So angry about society, yet passive about his own life situation. Strange, but whatever, I'm sick of it. Six months in this fucking booby hatch. I'm bored stiff. Pissed, frustrated, lonely. Horney, depressed. Fed up. Same shit every day. Sanding the shrink is a joke. No clue. And to top it off, Yip tells me that Mandy Milstein's getting out.

My man, Mr. Piano. Mr. Someone to watch over me. Mr. Movies. Mr. Fred Astaire and Ginger Rogers, finally getting out after thirty fucking months. The self-appointed "American Tragedy," out. It's hard to believe. What am I gonna do now? I mean, what? He's moving into his own apartment. He's going to graduate from Hartford in nine months, in the spring of '69. He's gonna play varsity shortstop. He's gonna be in the Thespian Club. He's gonna act in plays. He's even gonna direct plays, I hear. What? I even hear that he's gonna write a play. This guy is so fucking talented. He is one happening dude. I'm actually really happy for him, glad he's finally getting out. Getting to begin his life. Happy to know that people can succeed once they leave the loony bin. But, then again... What the fuck about me? Now, I'm really on my own. It's just Yip and me. And Yip can be boring after a while, O'Brian and Brian Boxman, they're the only ones left on Fuller II. No one to watch over me. Alone. You're on your own pal. I decide I gotta talk with Mandy Milstein tomorrow night at the social lounge.

The next night, walking into social lounge, there's MM sitting at the round table near the ice cream parlor surrounded by O'Brian and Boxman. They're hand slapping and congratulating Mandy. He's gone tomorrow. He's excited but trying to maintain his composure. He eyes me and waves me over to the table. I saunter over, trying for nonchalance. He continues with his news and his pep talk for

O'Brian, Boxman, and now me. The gang of five, minus one. The Yip, who always likes to stay back on the unit. Hardly ever goes outside, except to see his shrink. Yip of the gray pallor. He's back in the ward, as usual. Nothing personal, nothing against Mandy, I don't think. Just the Yip being Yip.

Mandy says, "Come on you guys, be happy for me, for Christ's sake. You know what, O'Brian, you're a pathetic specimen of Catholicism."

O'Brian: "Yeah, Mandy I guess you're right." Not much defense there, if anything a tone of defeat. "I'm not exactly inspiring the flock these days, huh?"

Mandy: "I'm hip. Hey Box. What's O'Brian's trip these days?"

Brian Boxman: "Beats me, Mandy. Some kind of simpering, depressive, wonked-out mood I guess."

O'Brian : "He's right Mandy. Just don't feel like doing much or feeling like much these days for that matter."

Mandy: "Give me a fucking break, Father. You are fucked. I don't give a fuck. This is my last night before I leave this fucking place and this is the best you can do? You can't even crack a smile for me. Fuck you. Hey, Arnie, you're his main man. What's O'Brian's trip?"

Me: "Come on you guys. You know you're taking the sarcasm thing a little far, don't you think? O'Brian's a hurting man. Can't be a fucking priest. Doesn't want to sell insurance. Wants to fuck women. Can't very well be a priest and do that shit. He's twisting."

Mandy: "Maybe you're right."

Me: "Maybe, we should show some respect and admiration for you. I mean you've been here for thirty fucking months and you're getting the fuck out. Actually, you're fucking thriving. Damn you're good, Mandy. But look, motherfucker. It ain't like that for the rest of us. Sorry to rain on your parade. Except maybe Brian here. He's gearing up, just like you, the motherfucker. College, baseball, college radio station announcer. He's getting ready, too. But O'Brian here and me, forget about the Yipster, we ain't that close."

Mandy: "Well, get that close. You can't wait for the fucking shrinks. You gotta fucking show 'em and tell 'em, man. They like your old man's money and they get off on talking to interesting, creative weirdos with more balls and heart than they got. They ain't in no hurry to be done with you. So, stop hanging back on your heels and do that Bobby Seale thing. Seize the day or do that Chambers Brothers' song and tell the shrinks, tell your old man, tell your old lady, social workers, too. Tell 'em you're ready. Tell 'em like the Chambers Brothers say, 'Time Has Come Today.' You're ready to get out. Don't you think you are, Arnie?"

Me: (feeling angry now): "Well, when you put it that way, yeah, I am. You know what, you're right. I am too passive. Letting this fucking depression, institutionalization, Thorazine control my ass. Forgot that. I have a will, and smarts, and perceptiveness, and toughness, and forget that. I'm as good as anybody. I can hang outside as good as anybody else out there. Yeah, Mandy. You're right. Ain't he father?"

Father O'Brian (half dead, halfhearted): "Uh huh. Yup, he is, Arnie."

Boxman: "You're probably right, Arnie. Mandy, here, he's feeling his oats today. Why not? Thirty months. Jesus fucking Christ. But you guys can't let yourselves be institutionalized like we did. I'm getting out in a couple of weeks after twenty fucking months, for Christ's sake. That's a fucking long time. That's almost two years out of my fucking life. Like O'Brian here, you're almost a year. You guys look like you're going backwards. This place will do that to you. Lull you into this lackadaisical, low-key rubber tit-like torpor. No stress, no challenge. No bueno. Gotta move the fuck on. You guys. I've been asleep for nineteen months. But I'm waking up. At last, next month, motherfucker, I'm gone, guys. You can be, too. Right, Father? Right, Arnie?"

Me: Definitely.

Father: "I guess so," in a low tone with lots of doubt in his voice.

Me: "Father, you're really going through it right now, aren't you? What to do with your life? I mean I'm only eighteen, but I sort of feel like I know what you're going through. Don't you, Box? Don't you, Mandy?"

Mandy: "Hey, I'm sorry, Father. I'm sorry for being so damn self-righteous. I mean, it's just been so long since things were going my way. I mean thirty months in this fucking place. Now, I'm feeling good again. I just sorta want everybody to feel this good, including you. You will. I'm sorry if I hurt your feelings, Father. I really am, Father."

Father: "That's O.K., Mandy. I know you and Box don't mean any harm. You're moving on, getting on with your life. And you want everybody to be in the same place as you. It'd be nice. It's just that I'm not. Arnie and me, we're kind of at ceiling zero. Actually, I feel like I'm below zero. Can't seem to pull out of it. Feel stuck. But I will though. Need to go out of the hospital some and try my hand at a job. Don't you think guys?"

"Yeah," we all agree.

Boxman: "Look Father, I did nineteen months in this joint. I was medicated up the yin yang, put on restrictions, caught smoking dope. Almost tried to hang myself my third month. But now that's over. See, I'm back. I'm back. And I'm better. I'm no different than you. Maybe a little younger. That's all. Look, we're both athletes. All of us actually. We're funny. Not bad looking guys, if you ask me. No homo. People like us. Girls. So what's the problem here? I don't get it. Whatever... I ain't looking back. I'm moving out next month. Me and Mandy are gonna be living together here in Hartford. I'm gonna complete college, play ball, just like Mandy. I'm gonna join the chess club. While, he's gonna be the William Powell of the Thespian Club, I'm gonna be the Bobby Fischer of the Chess Club. We're making it and we're gonna make it on the outside, too. Don't see why not. You, too."

Mandy: "You know, Father and Arnie, Box's right. You guys are as talented as we are, maybe more so. O'Brian, look at you man, you're thirty-eight , a great hitter, athletic, smart, funny, cool, literate, the ladies go wild for you. So what the fuck's the problem, man? You got just as much going for you as Box and me. And you, Arnie, I never saw anyone including me with as much all around talent as you. Brains, sports, smarts, funny, creative, amazing memory, sensitive, tough. I mean if anybody has it all, it's you, Arnie."

Me: "So what am I doing here then, Mandy?"

Mandy: "You know what, Arnie, I don't know if that question can really be answered. At least not now. It's too soon. We don't have enough historical distance yet. Maybe in twenty or thirty years, we'll have a clue. Now, we're too close to the experience. I mean that. I think it's true for all of us. I mean, look what's going on in the world right now. It's crazy. Who could have predicted it five years ago? I mean, revolution. Vietnam. Black Power. L.S.D. The country's in turmoil. There's really no accounting for it. But fuck it – I mean, you gotta hang in there even if we don't fully know why, or even if we don't really, truly know what's going on. We gotta fucking go on. And I swear it's good."

"I mean, I'm playing the best fucking shortstop of my career, straight A's. I love school. Got the lead in the school production of 'The Iceman Cometh.' Even the chicks are starting to come around. Look at Boxman. The man nearly offed himself three times before the IOL, once while in the IOL. Look at him. He's straight A'ing school, too. Playing grand master chess. Batting fourth, playing first on the Harford University baseball team. We're like this awesome combination. Who'd have predicted it after what he's been through? Just goes to show you, if not shows to go you. It can be done, motherfucker. But you gotta believe, and you gotta hang.

Arnie: "Mandy, Box, can we dispense with the goddamned pep talks for a fuckin' minute. Father and I are really glad for youse guys. We both think you're golden aces. You is. We gonna get there, too. I know that. But enough with the pep-talk sermon. It gets fucking old. Let's celebrate next month at your new pad, O.K.? I'm gonna try and get myself out of here now, too. You fucks is inspiring. But the fucking pep talks and sermons get boring. I think, I know what I have to do. Me and Father here, we gonna figure it out, get it together, do it and make like the motherfucking shepherd and get the flock out, Jack. Live happily after, all that jazz. Anyways, right on, Mandy. You the best. Don't worry 'bout us. We be fine. Boxman be looking after us for next month, right Box? Yip too, to the extent that he can. Fuckin' Yip. Yip, Box and me, we make sure Father, he O.K.

Box: "Yeah. And I'll make sure you and Father are O.K. before I move in with Mandy next month. And then we boogie in October at the new pad. O'day, Banky. Okay, dudes."

Father (sluggishly): "Cool."

Arnie: "Yup."

We four dudes finish up our chocolate fudge sundaes silently. Boxman and Milstein stand up without a word, slip out of the social lounge with a wave as they head out to the oval grass grounds, back to Fuller II for their afternoon naps. Father, leaves a minute later. He also goes back to Fuller II.

Alone at the table, I suddenly feel clear in my head. I feel energized, motivated. Alive for the first time in a long time. I can see the light at the end marking the beginning of the end of the tunnel. Endgame would now commence. Motherfucker, I think.

My hospital stay is now in my mind a chess game. Prep is over. Middle phase, it be gone, too. Six months, three weeks, endgame has begun. Loping back to my unit, Butler 1, I say hi to Yip and then exit to my bedroom. Lying down, face up to plan my leave legally and ethically, through channels. I think, nothing sleazy. Stay in control. Give 'em what they're looking for and what they want. Play the game. Behave and function. Get all the externals right and then they will have to release you. Demonstrate your self-control. Demonstrate your flexibility and mastery over your emotions. And then it's adios. Meet with your doctor, I say to myself. The next day, my regular time, I do.

Next day

Me: "Dr. Sanding. Good morning."

Sanding: "How are you?"

Me: "I'm fine. I want to talk with you about two things today. One is my progress. And two is my leaving date. I feel I am making good progress. I feel good. I'm starting to read again and study well. I think I'm ready to leave and go to college. I want to go to Ohio State. It starts in three weeks. I think I'm ready. My concentration is better. I am more engaged and involved with the activities around here. My energy is better. I'm sleeping well and I'm eating well. I don't know what else I need to do. I just feel like I'm ready. Six months is enough. I just don't think I need to be here anymore."

Sanding: "What about your folks, Arnie?"

Me: "What do you mean?"

Sanding: "I mean, have you discussed your plans with your folks?"

Me: "Not yet, Doc. I wanted to talk with you first."

Sanding: "Oh, well I see. What tells you that you can handle the rigors and challenges of college? I mean, it's pretty stressful for everyone. Not to mention someone who's been cooped up in a mental institution for six months."

Me: "I just told you. Doc. I feel good. I'm taking care of myself. Handling things. Handling school. Handling my homework. Getting my work done. I already have a high school diploma. I just think I'm ready to handle a full college load now. I want to go to Ohio State. "

Sanding: "Well, I think the school has said you're accepted and can start whenever you decide, either in September or January. What about January?"

Me: "Why not September?"

Sanding: "Isn't it kind of sudden? A little fast. I mean a month ago you were in North I, under constant supervision for starting a fire. Two months ago, you had a horrendous time at your senior prom and didn't even stay long enough to attend your graduation that weekend. Three and four months ago we were shooting you with Thorazine, practically daily, for acute anxiety. I mean, you haven't exactly been feeling good for very long. "

Me: "I know, but North I, I gotta tell you something's changed, Doc. I mean I feel like a new man. Energy's back. Concentration. I'm reading books again. I'm playing ball at the top of my game. I just feel like I'm back to my old self again, maybe better."

Sanding: "What about setbacks? You know going to college is a big adjustment for any kid. You know, leaving home. It's rough for everybody at times, and for you I think it's gonna be doubly hard. Not just getting used to college life, but getting used to being outside the Institute. I'm concerned that you could be setting yourself up. Why not wait until January? Give yourself a few more months to really get strong. Get some college credits under your belt here at the IOL through the University of Hartford and then give yourself a month at home back in New Rochelle to get used to the outside world again. And then after the Christmas holidays you go to Ohio. Why not do it that way? What do you say?"

Me: "Like, when do I get out then?"

Sanding: "I'm thinking the week of Thanksgiving. If everything goes all right, I don't see any reason at all why you couldn't go home for good the week of Thanksgiving. But everything has to go right. No more fires. You follow, Arnie?"

Me: "Yeah, I get it."

Sanding: "For one, no more fires. For two, you gotta just follow the rules. Go to school, keep taking good care of yourself, like how you've been doing. Keep going to group, keep seeing me. If you keep doing all those things like you've been doing , you'll be glad you waited."

Me (reluctantly): "Do I have a choice?"

Sanding: "Well , I'm not sure I would put it quite that way."

Me: "What way would you put it?"

Sanding: "Let's just say, I strongly suggest that you stick around here until Thanksgiving week in November and you'll leave here feeling really strong, really solid. Really ready."

Me (with half resignation): "Well, I, oh, okay. I mean, you're probably right, although I hate to admit it. Three months, huh? Hm, I can do three months standing on my head. All right, you win. I'll do it. Fuck it. What's three months anyway? The whole year's shot anyway, so..."

Sanding: "Yeah, and you'll get to ease into school instead of having to rush into it. Get a chance to relax at home and really be ready. Give yourself the best chance to really succeed."

Me: "Yeah. Yeah. Yeah. Ok. Three months. Then I 'm out of here. Is that a promise, Doc?"

Sanding: "Yes it is. And it's up to you but if you follow the ground rules. It's a promise."

And so the stage is set for the final campaign. Getting-to-know-you phase is over, working the shit through is over, so now it's time for endgame. The ball's finally in my court and I'm going to play a controlled offense. No slip ups. Only this time I'm gonna have some fun, too. You hear? I mean it this time. I'm not fucking kidding.

CHAPTER 38

Late September 1968

So the plan is launched. I'll take two college courses at the IOL this fall at the University of Hartford. Get my feet wet with college level material and get some credits as well. I figure my best bet is to go with my strong suits first. English and Western Civilization. B's and A's, my usual fare in these subjects. Makes sense to make life easy on myself. Who knows, maybe Sanding is right. Why should I rush it? Set myself up to fail and stuff. I kind of really hate to admit it. The guy is such a simp, ingenuous, pseudo-sensitive, "caring and kind." Ah, who knows, maybe he isn't such a bad guy after all.

I'm gonna get out in November. He promises me. As long as I keep my nose clean, keep my end of the bargain up, keep it together. No more fire-fuckups. No more of that sort of thing. I am motivated, finally beginning to see the light at the end of the tunnel. And the signal light is flashing yellow. Caution.

So going to class is part of the bargain. Homework. Reading. Keep attending your shrinkage appointments and before you know it, you'll be out. Adios Amigos. Okay Sanding, I'm in. So, college boy I am, trial run.

First day of class was even kind of fun. Mr. Gainsford, the instructor, is going all the way back. Back to Egypt. 6000 years. Way back. Kind of cool. There are five of us in the class. Two guys my age and three suburban housewife-types in their early forties, June, Sally and Lisa. All depressives, bridge players at the social lounge. Nice enough. Quiet, low-key. We exchange pleasantries. The guy my age, a hippie named Dave, has just arrived a month ago. He's at Fuller II. He's a Brooklynite who will play on our baseball team now that Mandy and Box are gone and living together near U of Hartford. Dave's moniker on the back of his baseball tee-shirt will be "Bad Trips." That's his unofficial patient-given diagnosis. He's entertaining. Has good stories. Loves the record "Crazy World of Arthur Brown" and the hit single "Fire. I'll teach you to burn."

Anywho, we're learning about the Pharaohs and early Egyptian social rituals and legal dictums set up in that ancient civilization. You know actually, after the first day, it's really boring. The instructor, Gaitsford, he's kind of dry. But I somehow manage to pay attention about half the time. A big improvement over my spring effort at the IOL classes, when I was finishing up high school. Then my concentration rate was about half this. When I'm spacing out, my thoughts go in two basic directions. One, Friendly's Ice Cream, the ice cream parlor and two, sex. I do my rotating girl fantasy of high school girls I used to know. Today, it is Greta, my friend from psych class and Pace college back in Mr. Satcher's class. She was hot, sharp and sassy. Liked to do it, too. Not that we ever did. But I sense in my mind that if I hadn't flipped out, that we might have. Anyway, thoughts of doing it with her help me get through the first couple of weeks in Western Civ.

Late one Tuesday morning in late September, or was it early October, on a clear, crisp powdery-blue-sky day, leaves pitter pattering off the trees, I'm walking out of class and there I spot a brunette wearing a Halloween orange colored miniskirt and black vest over a black turtleneck, walking out from the school toward her cottage. She's heading in that direction about the same time, as fortune will have it, as I am. Only as she walks, with a cute blonde about the same age, I can see that she is going, in about another hundred steps, to be walking in the opposite direction. She will be heading downhill toward the cottage on the campus green. While, in another hundred feet, I will be heading straight back into my unit. The two of them are walking slow. The blonde is pretty but not as foxy as the brunette. They are both carrying schoolbooks with their hands crossed over their chests. They have grins on their faces, as if laughing at some inside joke. I wonder what it is. Then, as they raise their heads from their chortling, they notice me. They wave. I wave back. I say "Hi." This a major developmental leap in my social skills at the IOL. They smile back, and the brunette says, "Hey, what's your name?"

"Arnie," I reply shyly, almost embarrassed. "What's yours?"

"Anita," the brunette says, plainly and without hesitation. The blonde quickly follows with, "I'm Julie. Are you in college?"

"Yeah," I say. "I just started three weeks ago."

"Oh, cool," Anita chimes in. "We're trying to get out of eleventh grade. Taking History, English, Trigonometry and Psychology. Man, it sucks."

Anita reaches into her black leather handbag for a Marlboro, gets one for Julie. And I simultaneously reach into my burnt sienna suede jacket and get a Viceroy. I take out my zippo lighter and we all light up.

Me: "How long you been here? I don't think I've seen you before," looking right at Anita and barely acknowledging the presence of Julie.

Anita: "We just got out of lock up. We've been here about two months. How about you?"

Me: "Seven months. Getting out though in November."

Anita: "Damn, really? I hate this place. Everyone here is so uptight. No freedom, always being watched. It's worse than home. At least at home, I could runaway."

Me: "You can here, too, you know. "

Anita: "Yeah, but they've been figuring I would do just that. So they kept me in lockup for the last two months. The fuckers. They just let me out yesterday. I've been taking classes while in lockup. Boy, that sucked. Kind of like being homeschooled. Now I gotta play the good girl routine to get anywhere. It's so phony. Right, Julie?"

Julie nods knowingly, takes a drag of her Marlboro then chimes in, "This fucking place SUCKS."

Me: "What are you in for?" (Looking at Julie)

Julie: "Cutting."

Me: "What?"

Julie: "You know."

Me: "Not sure."

Julie: "Cutting. You know, cutting my wrists."

Me: "Oh, you mean... trying to commit suicide."

Julie nods, with a slight blush, takes a deep drag.

I turn to Anita, feeling a little uncomfortable. Anita, getting the hint, "Usual bullshit, runaway from home, curfew shit, boyfriends, pot and drugs that stuff."

Me: "Out of control, huh?"

Anita: "Yeah... right. My fucked up parents didn't know how to deal with me. They were too busy drinking, having affairs and going to their stupid country club. Fucking hypocrites. I hate 'em. I hope they die." Julie nods approvingly.

Me: "You too, Julie?"

Julie: "Yeah, I hate my parents, especially my father, that fucker."

Me: "Quite a world we live in, huh?"

Anita: "You got that right, buster." Finishing her cigarette, she throws it onto the concrete walkway, stomps it out and, signaling to Julie says, "Well Arnold, I mean Arnie, nice meeting you. Gotta go. See you 'round campus, okay?"

Me: "Roger."

They scamper back toward their cottages. I hear intermittent cackles and giggles as I watch them, not sure if they are talking about me, and if they are whether it's approvingly or not. But mostly I'm staring at Anita's shapely calves and thighs, revealing themselves by virtue of her mini. I'm turned on.

I stand there for a minute more and then head back to my unit where I spy a guy I got to know down in North I. A regular mutate, Bill Peters. Your basic junkie, heroin-shooting, camel-smoking Bill. We nod and shake hands.

Me: "Good to see you man. When did you get here?"

Bill: "Just now. I just finished two months down there cleaning up from my habit. You know, withdrawal from skag. Feeling good. How 'bout you?"

Me: "I've been back over here from North I two months now, just starting college classes."

Bill: "Oh, really."

Me: "Yeah."

Bill: "Hey, by the way, did you happen to meet two girls named Julie and Anita while you were down there, by any chance?"

Me: "Just now actually. Why?"

Bill: "They are really cool. Anita balled me while I was down in North 1. The two sides got together one night, the boys' side and the girls' side, and we got together and escaped through the tunnels. She's something else. Loves to ball.

Me (Eyes popping out of my head): "Really?"

Bill: "Yeah, I want to get Julie, though. She's even foxier."

Me: "I don't think so."

Bill: "No? You like Anita better, huh?"

Me: "Yeah, definitely."

Bill: "Okay, you can have her. I'll take Julie. Maybe we'll both get laid."

Me: "Yeah, right. Not with my luck."

Bill: "Gotta think positive, kemosabe. Anyway, gotta get ready for lunch. Creamed kale, I hear. Shit on your basic shingle. Gourmet puke-fare."

Me: "Yeah, later."

I'm excited now. Gotta plan my approach. This time I will. I really will. Swirls of calmness, excitement and a nascent good feeling roll around my belly, putting me in a good mood. Kind of mellow. I go to my room and jerk off to some brunette with hot legs and fishnet stockings. Go to the lunchroom. Eat minimally of the shingle of shit being served. Eat the chocolate cake for dessert, then head back to my room for major after noon nappage.

Ten days Later

Walking out of class today only this time, it's just Anita there, no Julie. She's back at the cottage, sick or something. It's a dark, overcast fall day. Threatening rain. Anita's wearing a black slicker, black go-go boots, jet black thick hair, wavy. She wears it slightly above shoulder length. She waves at me out of the building as morning classes end and I walk over to her.

Me: "Hey. How ya' doin'?"

Anita (smiling, half mischievously): "Fine."

Me: "Where you off to?"

Anita: "You know, just back to the cottage."

Me: "Mind if I tag along?"

Anita: "Not at all. Gotta smoke?"

Me: "Sure." I pull out a Raleigh and give it to her and light it for her with my zippo. We walk silently for about twenty paces. "Bleak out here today."

Anita: "Bummer."

Me: "Where's Julie?"

Anita: "You know, like she's bummed, freaked out. Suicidal again and shit. They won't let her off the unit. Really, feeling edgy. Got that urge to cut herself again."

Me: "That's a drag."

Anita: "I'll tell you what, that ain't my trip."

Me: "Me neither." A twenty second pause then, "Yeah, so...what's happening today?"

Anita: "Well, not much." The two of us are now sauntering downhill on grass towards her cottage.

Anita: "Say, feel like getting loaded?"

Me: "Huh?" pretending I don't hear, to buy some time.

Anita: "You know, want to smoke some weed with me? I got some good Gold back in the cottage. Want to do some?"

Me, with a lot of hesitation: "Uh, um, okay. Sure, why not?"

Anita: "Cool. So, wait here and I'll be back in a minute, okay?"

Me: "All right," and Anita races to her cottage. I watch as she goes. Three minutes go by. I'm sweating, nervous, excited. It seems like an eternity. Finally, she darts out and we start walking away from the cottage at the far end of the campus, near the maintenance shed where the gardener's equipment is kept.

Anita: "Let's go behind the shed. It's quiet, protected. Nobody can see us here. We'll be safe okay?"

Me: "It's your party."

Anita: "Cool. I do this all the time."

Me: "Really?"

Anita: "Yeah, Julie and I go back here a lot and Bill and I did a couple of times."

Me: "Oh. Yeah. I know him. We hung out together on North I. Ex-junkie right?"

Anita: "That's him. He's cool though."

Me: "Yeah, I like him a lot. He said you guys used to go out."

Anita: "Yeah, but we're just friends now."

Me: "Ah, that's cool."

Anita, lighting up: "Get a hit of this."

Me, tentatively inhaling, trying but not succeeding to suppress a cough. Then coughing, sort of choking.

Anita, laughing, not unsympathetically, amused: "You're not used to getting stoned, huh?"

Me: "Yeah, it's been a while."

Anita: "That's cool."

Me: "I guess," toking again. This time, I barely cough.

Anita: "Really," toking deeply, then passing the J silently over to me.

Me: "Yup." I'm starting to feel the effects.

Anita, also starting to feel the effects, as the space between words grows longer, and time between speaking also gets longer. It's all on a sensory level now. Both the communication and perception, that is. It's clearly moved into a sensual vibe now. The eye contact, quick but intense, communicating lust. This is my sense, anyway. She's smiling for no apparent reason. We're stoned.

Finally, I say, " Yup. Here we are again."

Anita: "Um hm, feels good."

Me: "Yup."

Anita, cackling, moves sideways in my direction, seemingly to get away from the dirt and closer to the grass. I simultaneously move toward her. Inches apart now. Tense and intense. Vibes thick with expectancy, pleasure/pain sensations.

Me: Deep sigh.

Anita: "I'll drink to that," looking over to me in the same breath.

Me, I'm tingling. Leaping and lunging on her all at once, passionately kissing her on the lips, as we roll onto the dirt into a deep clinch, groin to groin. After half a minute of this, Anita is the first to speak.

Anita: "Whoosh, heavy."

Me: "Definitely."

Anita: "Mm, that was nice. Let's do that again. You're a good kisser. She kisses me sweetly this time, but that quickly becomes ardent. Then gets on top of me, simultaneously putting her hand on my fly as I reach behind her for her bra and discover for the first time that she hasn't been wearing one. YES.

Anita: "Let's do it. Okay? I'm on the pill. Let's do it. C'mon. Let's hurry. They're bound to see us."

I nod and she pulls my pants down and I pull her black tights and bikini underwear off. In a blur, the deed is done. I'm finally on the scoreboard. Goddammit. The two of us whirling and spinning, unclenched and entwined.

'Tis good, less a little dirt that creeps into some orifices. We rise, smoking our Marlboros and Raleighs, looking away.

Me: "Damn. This was the best time I have had in eight months.

Anita: "Yeah. Sex is fun, isn't it?"

Me: "Yeah, let's definitely do it again sometime, okay?"

Anita: "Sure, cool. You're a nice guy, I like you."

Me: "Yeah, I like you, too. No phony cock tease bullshit. Just straight forward, refreshing. I dig that.

Anita: "Thanks. You're cool yourself, guy."

Me, finishing my Raleigh: "Well, I guess I'll see you tomorrow. Okay. Good pot, good lovin', good day, my lady fair."

Anita: "Yes, sir. Glad to have been of service." We laugh and depart.

Seventh heaven revisited. I race back to my dorm. It's empty. They're all at lunch. I'm not hungry. I'm energized. I race off the unit and happily walk around the campus, doing the loop three times, looking for Yip, Father O'Brian. Anybody. I gotta tell somebody. This is so awesome. I'm stoked. I'm not even stoned anymore. Finally, after about three walks around, O'Brian appears alone, only with his pack of Larks to support him.

Me: "Hey, Father."

Father: "Yeah, Arnie."

Me: "Come here, Father."

Father: "What's up?"

Me: "You ain't gonna believe this."

Father: "What?"

Me: "You know, Anita de Blaine, that sixteen-year-old chick from the cottages who sometimes walks around the campus when we do?"

Father: "Oh, you mean the pretty brunette teenybopper hippie girl."

Me: "Yeah, that's her."

Father: "What about her?"

Me: "Guess what we were just doin'?"

Father: "You're kiddin' me."

Me: "I swear to God. Got loaded, too. Do you believe that shit, father?"

Father: "Damn, Arnie. You're something else, man. That's tremendous. You're living up to your nickname now. Horney Arnie."

Me: "Yeah, I guess I am. I'm so fucking stoked, Father. Damn, man. I really didn't think it was possible to feel good. But guess what, man, it is. Sex, drugs and rock 'n' roll. There's a reason this shit is dangerous. People feel good doing that stuff. No wonder the older generation can't stand the stuff, it's too fucking pleasurable."

Father: "Arnie, you know what, I think you're right. Who else knows?"

Me: "No one. Just you. You're the only one who is hearing my confession father," (jokingly).

Father: "Cool, let's keep it that way. You know how word gets around."

Me: "Yeah, definitely."

Father: "Anyways, I wanted to tell you that Mandy Millstein is doing great and Brian Boxman has just moved in with him. Been there about two weeks now. He seems revved."

Me: "I'll bet. Lucky dog. Two more months or less for me now, Father. How 'bout you?"

Father: "As soon as I finish up this insurance sales thing and make a decision, I'm going back to Buffalo."

Me: "How's that going, Father?"

Father: "Ah, I'm still on the fence. I got twenty years tied into the priesthood. All this time, energy, money and commitment. It's not easy. Still, the secular world does have its appeals, as you can attest. Right, Arnie?"

Me: "I reckon so. Anyway, keep me posted, will you? And let me know if you see Mandy and Box. Those fucking bastards. You get to go off campus. I don't. But you know what? I'm gonna start, Father."

Father: "Getting adventurous, huh, Arn?"

Me: "Kind of. "

Father: "Okay, but just be careful. You don't want to blow your discharge date. November isn't a long time from now. I mean November 26 is only fifty-two days away. Play it cool, okay?"

Me: "You know me, Father. Mr. Cool Hand Luke himself."

Father: "Okay, Arnie. Anyway, I gotta head out to volleyball. Get some exercise. You know, volleyball and ping-pong and a lot of dandy games. That's what we got here. Yes, siree. Yes, siree. Anywho, we'll see you."

Me, nodding: "Yes you will. Yes you will."

CHAPTER 39

October 1968, One Month later

Behind that maintenance shed after class, Anita and I are going at it. It's our fifth time. Who's counting? Stoned and lustoleum. It's doing wonders for my head. Only O'Brian knows about it. The shrinks don't have a clue. If they do, they 'ain't talkin'. We're pretty careful. Only Anita's friend Julie knows. And she's not apt to squeal, as Anita would report her for the pot she keeps hidden. As fun as it is, it's starting to get old. I begin to realize there isn't much dialogue with her pre or post coitus. It's your basic stoned roll in the hay routine. Starting to get stale. Anita is looking bored too. After a session, she looks up at me from the prone position.

Anita: "How can you stand it here?"

Me: "I can't. But I'm getting out."

Anita: "I'm never getting out. My parents don't really want me back. They're getting divorced anyway. I'm only in the way. I'm thinking of heading to San Francisco."

Me: "Really?"

Anita: "Yeah, want to come? It 'll be fun. We can live in the Haight, in a commune. We'll have a blast."

Me: "Mm, it sure is tempting. I've been wanting to go out there for a long time. Since I saw the "Maltese Falcon" on T.V. You know, the old Bogart film. It takes place in San Francisco in the 30's. Hmm. It's really tempting, I gotta admit. How would we get there? "

Anita: "I dunno. Greyhound. I can't drive."

Me: "Yeah, I haven't driven since the breakdown. I think I'd be a little gun-shy driving 3,000 miles. Greyhound, huh? Hmm, it's so fucking tempting." I contemplate it in silence for another twenty seconds or so. "I dunno. You know, I really want to go to college. I already am a quarter behind the other people.

Everyone in my class started in the fall. I hate that. No, as groovy as I think goin' to SF would be, I gotta go to school. Hope you don't mind."

Anita: "Nah, well I am a little disappointed. It would be fun to go there with you. But, fuck it, I'm gonna go anyway. Fucking Julie, she's pretty useless. I ain't gonna go out there with her. She's too screwed up to go. She's probably gonna kill herself one of these days. I can't hack that shit."

Me: "Yeah, I can't blame you."

Anita: "Anyways, don't be surprised if you hear about my AWOL soon. And don't you dare tell, you hear?"

Me: "All right. Just do me a favor."

Anita: "What?"

Me: "Just be careful. Watch your ass. And I mean that literally."

Anita: "Yeah, yeah, yeah. Thanks, Dad."

Me: "I ain't shittin' you."

Anita: "Yeah, yeah, yeah."

Me: "Okay, smart ass. Forget I said anything. Okay, just forget it."

Anita: "You know what. You're great. Now, you remember that. Hear? You remember that, and you'll be fine, my friend."

Me: "Yeah. Okay, Ma. You, too. You remember that, too. All right."

Anita: "I know, I will. Well, you know what? It's been fun, smoking dope and getting high with you. Oh yeah, and don't let me forget, the ballin'. That's been super fun too."

Me: "Back at you."

So, we both get up from the shed and make our way back to our respective "dorms," Anita to her cottage, and me, back to my unit. Strangely content. Complete. Even if not exactly fully satisfied. Sex isn't the whole enchilada, I think to myself. Anita, she's hot and kind of nice. But she's too young, kind of a wild child. Fun, maybe kind of smart, but not that informed. I dunno. Something missing there. Not the sex part, that's for sure, but maybe something else. Maybe something mental.

I run back to Butler in a strange, new but not altogether unpleasant state of perplexed. I go straight to my room as once again, there really isn't anyone on the floor of the unit to talk to, or anyone who I want to talk to. So, back to the bed. I put on my new Simon and Garfunkel album, the one that's just come out: "Bookends." I like it. This is my third time listening to it. One of those albums that grows on you – but fast. Some albums grab you the first time, like "Sgt. Pepper's." Some never grab you at all, some don't grab you until someone explains it to you, like "John Wesley Harding," the relatively new country Dylan album that just came out. Very symbolic, even religious. Or at least that's what the Yipster explained to me. He's so fucking well-read and knowledgeable about literary shit. It's fucking inspiring.

No, "Bookends" is one of those that takes about three or four listens. Good record. I love the song "America" the best. Kind of describes what I want to do. Kind of sad. Kind of political. Describes the mood of my generation, lost in America. Not the country I grew up in. Different since the Kennedy assassination and the Beatles. I fall asleep as the album ends on side two.

> "Old friends, old friends,
> Sat on their park bench like bookends."

Napping out in dreamland for three hours. Only to wake up, mostly refreshed.

The next day, I earn my first pass off campus. It only took me eight and half months almost. I'm off to Mandy and Brian's pad near the University of Hartford campus, where the two of them are living in a two bedroom apartment. They're both in a jovial mood. The three of us eat scrambled eggs and salami in their little kitchen nook off the living room, pick up a football lying on the kitchen counter and take a jaunt to the street for a three-way football catch. The vibe from them is exuberant and jubilant. I am buoyed by their enthusiasm. One month to go.

Milstein talks of his role as Hickey in the upcoming production of "The Iceman Cometh." He got the starring role. That was quick. And he talks hurriedly about how he has been utilizing his hospital experience to help him prepare for the part both in his head and in the early rehearsals. The down and out shit he has witnessed and experienced at the IOL has provided him with ample material that he can use to access the character of the salesman, Hickey, the part I saw on T.V. being played by the great Jason Robards. Mandy says it's easy to tap into the depressing, fucked-up, down and out ambience of Harry Hope's dive bar where the whole play takes place. He simply thinks he's at the IOL when he's playing the part. It's a more than ample place to go in his head, he says. He certainly feels that the IOL has given him the depth to play the part. In spades. No lacking for depth here is what he says kind of proudly, as if he's found a way to use the experience of the past two and a half years positively.

As we're walking to the park a few blocks away, Boxman goes into a riff about how the new chess moves he mastered has put him right in the cross hairs of the number one chess guy on the chess team at college. He talks as if he has no doubt at all that he will soon knock off the number one guy and be the king of the hill. I listen excitedly and am turned on by his confidence. I believe him. I've seen Boxman play on a few occasions. Guy is uncanny. Like he knows what you're gonna do before you do it. Thinks three or four moves ahead. I don't know how he does it. Amazing. Him and Mandy. Both these guys are so fucking talented I think. They say it too about me but I play it off with some degree of genuine modesty when I do. As if, who really gives a shit? More fun to do the stuff than to get into an ego trip about it is what I get from their attitudes.

I mostly listen when I'm with these guys. They're kind of my mentors. I hardly mention my "trip" except to say that I'm looking forward to getting out, which hardly needs mentioning. It's so great hanging with the two of them. Relaxing. I can really be myself. No pressure. No need to pretend I'm anything other than who I am or how I'm feeling at any given moment. If I'm depressed, so be it. Anxious, so be it. Pissed, so be it. All cool with them. They've been there. No need to explain. No need to apologize. No need to hide it at least on their behalf. Awesome. These guys, Father O'Brian, Yip, even the Fox, although he's long gone. These are really the first people in my whole life with whom I could really be completely myself. It's a great feeling.

After our walk to the park and more football catches there, we go back to their pad and decide to plan a baseball game in late November to celebrate the harvest and more importantly, my discharge. We assign Father O'Brian the job of coordinating a game with the young shrinks - a grudge match. This really excites me.

We part until the next month's farewell softball finale. I leave their place with a warm feeling and a deepening conviction in the possibility of health, healing and even happiness. YES. I clench my fist inward in the Black Power way I've seen Stokely Carmichael do in speeches. It's now being emulated by the Black Panthers, a new radical group from Oakland, California that I've also heard about from the news on T.V. I'm stoked. Really starting to feel good. So relieving. But alas... The news isn't good on all fronts.

Three days later, I get word O'Brian has gone into a deep, almost catatonic depression. Physically, really stiff. Tight. Speech slurred, hard to decipher, low talking voice. Looking down with that scared look in his eye. Ashamed to look you in the eye. Really down. Reduced to one word answers again. Can't really say why. Looks almost tearful. It's really sad. I hear from the Yipster that his monsignor has given him a deadline. Decide what it's gonna be. Priesthood or insurance broker. One or the other. You gotta choose. But you better do it quick, 'cuz we're pulling the financial plug at the end of November.

O'Brian's really feeling the pressure, Yipster thinks. Although, you can hardly surmise it from the amount of talk coming out of the Father's mouth these days. But Yip, he knows the score. O'Brian looks like he's crumbling under the weight. Selling insurance is not really in his heart in the way that being a priest has been in a lot of ways. But he can't and doesn't really want to suppress his appetites for wine, women and song, as he puts it either.

He feels stuck and I feel rotten for the guy. Almost guilty for how well I feel and for how well Boxman and Milstein are doing. But I tell myself that I can't let myself get sucked in. I just can't. I try to hold the emotional line. It's not easy. I feel for people I like and love. I can't help it. I just do. But I try. And this time, I succeed in putting my caring feelings on the shelf. It's not easy. I have to distract myself with a lot of T.V., football games, records and Raleigh cigarettes. I stop smoking dope. That's a pathway into my feelings. And right now I need to keep my feelings in some kind of check. It works, for a change. It takes determination and effort. Even though I identify with, and can relate to O'Brian's sadness and pain, I don't let myself get dragged down. It works. O'Brian stops coming out of his unit for walks on the campus green. I only hear news from his roommates up on Fuller. It's not good news. But I go on.

And then, one week later, walking back from the Lounge and the mandatory root beer float that I always order there, I run into Yip hurriedly rushing towards me. With bated breath, he puts an arm around my shoulder, a somewhat unusual move for him. In hushed tones he whispers, "Arndris, I have to tell you something."

Me: "What?" Seeing the look on Yip's face I know it ain't good. "What? Spill it."

Yip: "Arndris... Boxman's... dead!

Me: "What?" shocked, stunned.

Yip: "He shot himself last night."

Me: "Why?"

Yip: "Nobody knows."

Me: "Mandy?"

Yip: "He found him. He's freaked out, majorly. But he's all right."

Me: "God."

Yip: "Yeah I know. It's awful Arndris. He fooled everybody. Mandy, the shrinks, me. He made everyone think he was fine. That fucker."

Me: "This can't be. That guy was the picture of health. I just saw him. He couldn't fool me. I know when people are faking it.

Yip: "That guy was a better actor than Mandy Milstein, Foxy, you and me combined. He was so good he conned himself."

Me: "This is too much. I gotta get out of here."

Yip: "You will, Arndris."

Me: "Yes. I will. Fuck."

Yip: "Ok, Arndris. Now, you gotta settle down. You hear. Take it easy. I have been through this before. Both here and back in NYC. You'll get through this, too. I'll help you."

Me: "Okay."

Yip: "You and me, Arndris."

Me: "Me and you, Yip."

We smoke about six cigarettes a piece and head back to the unit, steeled. The next day my shrink informs me that I'm going home in twenty-one days. He's impressed with my progress, and how I'm doing in all phases, especially with how I seem to be handling Boxman's suicide. Method acting kicking in. No help from him. Yip guides me through the somatic, emotional and imagistic aspects of the internal experience of dealing with the death of someone you care about, as we use each other to help regain our balance. Yip is mostly the teacher, the guide. We do it in two three-hour rap sessions, just him and me, on the unit, on walks, on the campus, in his room, in mine. Away from the professionals. Barely discuss it with the shrink. Barely mention it in group therapy. Barely mention to the nurses on the unit. Just the Yipster and me.

We move on. Boxman is buried in his hometown of Clearwater, Florida. It seems he lost the chess match to the number one guy at the university. That's the best Mandy Milstein can come up with when I speak with him on the phone. It seems improbable that's all there was to it. How little we know, I think. How little we know one another. Really. Deep down. Even people we trust, care for and think are being honest with us, I think. That fucking prick, I also think. Goddamn it. I really cared about that guy. Pushing away tears of sadness, tears of rage. Yip and I talk every day for about five days, a couple of hours every day. Kind of a parallel therapy, only for real. We schmooze it out.

When the dream came
I held my breath
With my eyes closed
I went insane,
Like a smoke ring day
When the wind blows
Now I won't be back

Till later on

If I do come back at all

~ Neil Young. On the Way Home. Buffalo Springfield.

"Last Time Around" 1968. Side one. Song one.

CHAPTER 40

On the Way Home

Sunday, November 24th. Morning. It is one of those perfect New England fall days. Clear blue sky, puffy cumulus clouds. Crisp, blowy, high 40's weather. Football weather. But today, baseball is on the bill of fare. Yip is up early. It's 8:00 a.m. He's got on his powder blue terry cloth robe, Camel nonfilters in tow. Yankee cap. Baseball glove. He's ready. Tongue clucking like a hen. Jazzed.

I'm expectant, too. Yip and I smoke a few cigarettes after breakfast and then it's time to go and meet Milstein. We meet O'Brian and walk three blocks to the local park. There we meet Milstein and his new roommate, Lem, our pitcher, who was released about a week ago, Boxman's replacement.

As we're walking over to the park, Yip tells me that his shrink plans to play. I'm not sure if the Sandman's gonna make it. I hope so. But I have my doubts. We'll see.

Arriving at the park, we see the ballpark and there's a bevy of sweat-shirted men and a couple of women in the distance.

They're tossing balls around and a guy who I can't quite make out is fungoing balls to infielders, getting their practice in.

Getting closer to the field, I spy Mandy Milstein and he's talking to none other than Dr. Sanding. The man has shown up. They're discussing ground rules. Flipping for first ups. Sanding nods as he sees me and waves warmly. I wave shyly at first and then with an edge of bravado, purse my lips, pick up a ball and throw it to O'Brian with an air of nonchalance. "Come on," I yell to Mandy. "Let's get this thing going."

We win the coin toss and we're up last. Mandy calls out, "Let's get in the field. Arnie, you're in left. Father, you're on first. Lem, you're pitching."

And the rest of us "Mutated Psychotics," as our team is called, takes the field. Mandy assumes his position at shortstop. Five shrinks, one male RN, and three data processing guys make up the opposing team. They call themselves, rather creatively, "Data Processing." We call them the "Normal Paths."

Sanding leads off. He tries to hit it out but gets under it and hits a loping fly ball to me. One out. Mandy's shrink grounds tepidly to first. Data Processing, Lem, their slugger, hits a line drive right to O'Brian. Three up. Three down. Milstein leads off. Doubles down the left field line. Me, first pitch, a change up, into right center. One run in, I stop at second with a double. O'Brian, temporarily out of his depression, uncorks one to deep right. Two runs coming in. The score is 3–0.

So it goes. No contest really. After five innings, its 7–0. Lem is pitching a two-hitter. We'll play nine. Sanding hits a scorcher past third in the sixth. I race over from left to the line to retrieve the ball, he darts around second without hesitation heading to third. I whirl fire to Mandy covering third, a one-bouncer, which Mandy scoops up with his glove, and in the same motion tags Sanding in the nose, pretty hard. You're out. The umpire calls. Their last threat.

They go down feebly in the ninth. Final score, 9–0. A two-hitter for Lem. Psychotomutates – victorious. Congratulations, handshakes all round, exits to cars by the opposing team. Sanding, pleasantly and humbly approaches me after the game.

"Great throw, Arnie. I guess you taught your old shrink a lesson about the dangers of running on the arm of a soon to-be- graduate of the IOL."

Huh, I'm thinking, not expecting this reaction.

"Great throw. Great win. You guys were great."

What can I say? So magnanimous in defeat, I admit. He really is happy that our team and I did so well. He actually did seem glad for me. I search but could not find any competitive disgust or disappointment in his vibe. Damn it. I thought. I guess that not everyone is so competitive to the core. I sure am. But somehow, he's okay with our win. Anyway, it was a great win. I am mildly disappointed that my shrink isn't humiliated by their loss, I guess in the same way that I want to humiliate my father on his own terms (winning). But maybe there are things more important than winning. I don't know.

After the game is over it's just the five of us Mutates left. Lem, our winning pitcher and Mandy's new roommate, O'Brian, Yip, Mandy and me. Huddled around the home plate, Mandy and Lem drinking beer, we pause.

In two days, I will be leaving. The game. The weather. This day. It has perfection to it. Losers win. Baseball in November. Comrades in arms coming together in memory of our fallen comrade. I don't know. All of that, somehow. There is a beauty to this day. Mostly, there is a feeling of recognition. Of an ending. An ending of my incarceration. The end of my childhood. The beginning of the reckoning with the darkness. The darkness of the unknown of life, inside and out. The knowledge of aloneness. Isolation, tempered with the power and consolation provided by friends in communion, struggles, suffering, cajoling, prodding, but always hanging. Hanging in there. Sometimes, by our thumbs. And then there will be more understanding, not platitudinizing, soft sudsing or making it any heavier than it needs to be.

We are 60's casualties. Veterans of the internal wars, given a second chance to regroup-recoup. O'Brian, finally making up his mind. Giving the old college try to life insurance. Leaving the priesthood. Finally. Mandy Milstein graduating the following June with a degree in theatre to become a Broadway actor, director and playwright. Yip, to stay a patient another six months and then, having had enough of the same old same old, off to California where he puts his money where his mouth is, going off to work with Cesar Chavez and the United Farm Workers. Lastly, there's me.